— ★ —

BODY IN QUESTION

I reached in and pulled at the corner of the pillow-case, gingerly working it back and forth, trying not to disturb its contents. But finally I had to pull it off altogether, and the thing that had been in the pillowcase rolled onto its side.

A skull grinned up at me.

"Oh, my God," I said, slamming the lid down and sitting on the seat, covering my face with both trembling hands. The next minute I was in frantic action, lowering those blinds, checking to make sure the front door was locked, finding the light switch, and flipping on the overhead light in the suddenly darkened room.

I opened the window seat again, hoping its contents had miraculously changed.

The skull still lay there with its slack-jawed grin.

Then the doorbell rang.

— ★ —

"... the ultimate clue is a marvelous take-off on a classic one."

—Murder ad lib

Also available from Worldwide Mystery by
CHARLAINE HARRIS

REAL MURDERS

A BONE TO PICK

Charlaine Harris

WORLDWIDE ®

TORONTO • NEW YORK • LONDON
AMSTERDAM • PARIS • SYDNEY • HAMBURG
STOCKHOLM • ATHENS • TOKYO • MILAN
MADRID • WARSAW • BUDAPEST • AUCKLAND

A BONE TO PICK

A Worldwide Mystery/January 1994

This edition is reprinted by arrangement with Walker and Company.

ISBN 0-373-26136-5

Printed in U.S.A.

For Patrick, Timothy and Julia

ONE

In less than a year, I went to three weddings and one funeral. By late May (at the second wedding but before the funeral) I had decided it was going to be the worst year of my life.

The second wedding was actually a happy one from my point of view, but my smile muscles ached all the next day from the anxious grin I'd forced to my lips. Being the daughter of the bride felt pretty peculiar.

My mother and her fiancé strolled between the folding chairs arranged in her living room, ended up before the handsome Episcopalian priest, and Aida Brattle Teagarden became Mrs. John Queensland.

In the oddest way, I felt my parents had left home while I had stayed. My father and his second wife, with my half brother Phillip, had moved across the country to California in the past year. Now my mother, though she'd still be living in the same town, would definitely have new priorities.

That would be a relief.

So I beamed at John Queensland's married sons and their spouses. One of the wives was pregnant—my mother would be a stepgrandmother! I smiled graciously at Lawrenceton's new Episcopal priest, Aubrey Scott. I oozed goodwill at the real estate salespeople from my mother's business. I grinned at my best friend, Amina Day, until she told me to relax.

"You don't have to smile every second," she whispered from one corner of her mouth, while the rest of her face paid respectful attention to the cake-cutting ceremony. I instantly rearranged my face into more sober lines, thankful beyond expression that Amina had been able to get a few days off from her job in Houston as a legal secretary. But later, at the reception, she told me my mother's wedding wasn't her only reason for coming back to Lawrenceton for the weekend.

"I'm getting married," she said shyly, when we found a corner to ourselves. "I told Mamma and Daddy last night."

"To—which one?" I said, stunned.

"You haven't been listening to a word I said when I called you!"

Maybe I *had* let the specifics roll over me like a river. Amina had dated so many men. Since she'd reached fourteen, her incredible dating career had only been interrupted by one brief marriage.

"The department store manager?" I pushed my glasses back up on my nose the better to peer up at

Amina, who is a very nice five feet, five inches. On good days I say I am five feet.

"No, Roe," Amina said with a sigh. "It's the lawyer from the firm across the hall from the place I work. Hugh Price." Her face went all gooey.

So I asked the obligatory questions: how he'd asked her, how long they'd dated, if his mother was tolerable . . . and the date and location of the ceremony. Amina, a traditionalist, would finally be married in Lawrenceton, and they were going to wait a few months, which I thought was an excellent idea. Her first wedding had been an elopement with myself and the groom's best friend as incompatible attendants.

I was going to be a bridesmaid again. Amina was not the only friend I'd "stood up" for, but she was the only one I'd stood up for twice. How many times could you be bridesmaid to the same bride? I wondered if the last time I came down the aisle ahead of Amina I would have to use a walker.

Then my mother and John made their dignified exit, John's white hair and white teeth gleaming, and my mother looking as glamorous as usual. They were going to honeymoon for three weeks in the Bahamas.

My mother's wedding day.

I GOT DRESSED for the first wedding, the January one, as though I was putting on armor to go into battle. I braided my bushy, wavy brown hair into a sophisticated (I hoped) pattern on the back of my head, put on the bra that maximized my most visible assets, and slid a brand-new gold-and-blue dress with padded shoulders over my head. The heels I was going to wear were ones I'd gotten to go with a dress I'd worn on a date with Robin Crusoe, and I sighed heavily as I slid my feet into them. It had been months since I'd seen Robin, and the day was depressing enough without thinking of him. At least the heels probably hiked me up to five foot two. I put on my makeup with my face as close to the illuminated mirror as I could manage, since without my glasses I can't make out my reflection very well. I put on as much makeup as I felt comfortable with, and then a little more. My round brown eyes got rounder, my lashes got longer, and then I covered them up with my big, round tortoiseshell glasses.

Sliding a precautionary handkerchief into my purse, I eyed myself in the mirror, hoped I looked dignified and unconcerned, and went down the stairs to the kitchen of my townhouse apartment to gather up my keys and good coat before sallying forth to that most wretched of obligatory events, the Wedding of a Recent Former Boyfriend.

Arthur Smith and I had met through a club we both attended, Real Murders. He'd helped on the homicide investigation that had followed the murder of one of the club members, and the string of deaths that followed this initial murder. I'd dated Arthur for months after the investigation was over, and our relationship had been my only experience of a red-hot romance. We sizzled together, we became something more than a nearly thirty librarian and a divorced policeman.

And then, as suddenly as the fire had flared, it died out, but on his side of the hearth first. I had finally gotten the message—"I'm continuing this relationship until I can figure out a way to get out without a scene"—and with an immense effort I'd gathered my dignity together and ended our relationship without causing that scene. But it had taken all my emotional energy and willpower, and for maybe six months I'd been crying into my pillow.

Just when I was feeling better and hadn't driven past the police station in a week, I saw the engagement announcement in the *Sentinel*.

I saw green for envy, I saw red for rage, I saw blue for depression. I would never get married, I decided, I would just go to other people's weddings the rest of my life. Maybe I could arrange to be out of town the weekend of the wedding so I wouldn't be tempted to drive past the church.

Then the invitation came in the mail.

Lynn Liggett, Arthur's fiancée and fellow detective, had thrown down the gauntlet. Or at least that's how I interpreted the invitation.

Now, in my blue-and-gold and my fancy hairdo, I had grasped it. I'd picked out an impersonal and expensive plate in Lynn's pattern at the department store and left my card on it, and now I was going to the wedding.

The usher was a policeman I knew from the time I dated Arthur.

"Good to see you," he said doubtfully. "You look great, Roe." He looked stiff and uncomfortable in his tux, but he offered his arm properly. "Friend of the bride, or friend of the groom?" he asked automatically, and then flushed as red as a beet.

"Let's say friend of the groom," I suggested gently, and gave myself high marks. Poor Detective Henske marched me down the aisle to an empty seat and dumped me with obvious relief.

I glanced around as little as possible, putting all my energy into looking relaxed and nonchalant, sort of as if I'd just happened to be appropriately dressed and just happened to see the wedding invitation on my way out the door, and decided I'd just drop in. It was all right to look at Arthur when he entered, everyone else was. His pale blond hair was crisp and curly and short, his blue eyes as direct and engaging as ever. He was wearing a gray tux and he looked great. It didn't hurt *quite* as much as I'd thought it would.

When the "Wedding March" began, everyone rose for the entrance of the bride, and I gritted my teeth in anticipation. I was pretty sure my fixed smile looked more like a snarl. I turned reluctantly to watch Lynn make her entrance. Here she came, swathed in white, veiled, as tall as Arthur, her straight, short hair curled for the occasion. Lynn was almost a foot taller than I, something that had obviously bothered her, but I guessed it wasn't going to bother her anymore.

Then Lynn passed me, and when I saw her in profile I gasped. Lynn was clearly pregnant.

It would be hard to say why this was such a blow; I certainly hadn't wanted to become pregnant while I was dating Arthur, and would have been horrified if I'd been faced with the situation. But I had often thought of marrying him, and I had occasionally thought about babies; most women my age, if they do want to get married, do think about babies. Somehow, just for a little while, it seemed to me that I had been robbed of something.

I spoke to enough people on the way out of the church to be sure my attendance registered and would be reported to the happy couple, and then I skipped the reception. There was no point in putting myself through that. I thought it was pretty stupid of me to have come at all; not gallant, not brave, just dumb.

THE FUNERAL CAME THIRD, a few days after my mother's wedding, and, as funerals go, it was pretty decent. Though it was in early June, the day Jane Engle was buried was not insufferably hot, and it was not raining. The little Episcopal church held a reasonable number of people—I won't say mourners, because Jane's passing was more a time to be marked than a tragic occasion. Jane had been old, and, as it turned out, very ill, though she had told no one. The people in the pews had gone to church with Jane, or remembered her from her years working in the high school library, but she had no family besides one aging cousin, Parnell Engle, who was himself too ill that day to come. Aubrey Scott, the Episcopal priest, whom I hadn't seen since my mother's wedding, was eloquent about Jane's inoffensive life and her charm and intelligence; Jane had certainly had her tart side, too, but the Reverend Mr. Scott tactfully included that under "colorful." It was not an adjective I would have chosen for silver-haired Jane, never married—like me, I reminded myself miserably, and wondered if this many people would come to my funeral. My eyes wandered over the faces in the pews, all more or less familiar. Besides me, there was one other attendee from Real Murders, the disbanded club in which

Jane and I had become friends—LeMaster Cane, a black businessman. He was sitting at the back in a pew by himself.

I made a point of standing by LeMaster at the graveside, so he wouldn't look so lonely. When I murmured that it was good to see him, he replied, "Jane was the only white person who ever looked at me like she couldn't tell what color I am." Which effectively shut me up.

I realized that I hadn't known Jane as well as I thought I had. For the first time, I really felt I would miss her.

I thought of her little, neat house, crammed with her mother's furniture and Jane's own books. I remembered Jane had liked cats, and I wondered if anyone had taken over the care of her gold tabby, Madeleine. (The cat had been named for the nineteenth-century Scottish poisoner Madeleine Smith, a favorite murderer of Jane's. Maybe Jane had been more "colorful" than I'd realized. Not many little old ladies I knew had favorite murderers. Maybe I was "colorful," too.)

As I walked slowly to my car, leaving Jane Engle forever in Shady Rest Cemetery—I thought—I heard someone calling my name behind me.

"Miss Teagarden!" panted the man who was hurrying to catch up. I waited, wondering what on earth he could want. His round, red face topped by thinning light brown hair was familiar, but I couldn't recall his name.

"Bubba Sewell," he introduced himself, giving my hand a quick shake. He had the thickest southern accent I'd heard in a long time. "I was Miss Engle's lawyer. You are Aurora Teagarden, right?"

"Yes, excuse me," I said. "I was just so surprised." I remembered now that I'd seen Bubba Sewell at the hospital during Jane's last illness.

"Well, it's fortunate you came today," Bubba Sewell said. He'd caught his breath, and I saw him now as he undoubtedly wanted to present himself; an expensively suited, sophisticated but down-home man in the know. A college-educated good ole boy. His small brown eyes watched me sharply and curiously. "Miss Engle had a clause in her will that is significant to you," he said significantly.

"Oh?" I could feel my heels sinking into the soft turf and wondered if I'd have to step out of my shoes and pull them up by hand. It was warm enough for my face to feel damp; of course, my glasses began to slide down my nose. I poked them back up with my forefinger.

"Maybe you have a minute now to come by my office and talk about it?"

I glanced automatically at my watch. "Yes, I have time," I said judiciously after a moment's pause. This was pure bluff, so Mr. Sewell wouldn't think I was a woman with nothing to do.

Actually, I very nearly was. A cutback in funding meant that, for the library to stay open the same number of hours, some staff had to go part-time. I hoped it was because I was the most recently hired that the first one to feel the ax was me. I was only working eighteen to twenty hours a week now. If I hadn't been living rent free and receiving a small salary as resident manager of one of Mother's apartment buildings (actually a row of four town houses), my situation would have been bleak in the extreme.

Mr. Sewell gave me such elaborate directions to his office that I couldn't have gotten lost if I'd tried, and he furthermore insisted I follow him there. The whole way he gave turn signals so far in advance that I almost made the wrong left once. In addition he would wave and point into his rearview mirror, waiting to see me nod every time in acknowledgment. Since I'd lived in Lawrenceton my whole life, this was unnecessary and intensely irritating. Only my curiosity about what he was going to tell me kept me from ramming his rear, and then apologizing picturesquely with tears and a handkerchief.

"Wasn't too hard to find, was it!" he said encouragingly when I got out of my car in the parking lot of the Jasper Building, one of the oldest office buildings in our town and a familiar landmark to me from childhood.

"No," I said briefly, not trusting myself to speak further.

"I'm up on the third floor," Lawyer Sewell announced, I guess in case I got lost between the parking lot and the front door. I bit the inside of my lip and boarded the elevator in silence, while Sewell kept up a patter of small talk about the attendance at the funeral, how Jane's loss would affect many, many people, the weather, and why he liked having an office in the Jasper Building (atmosphere...much better than one of those prefabricated buildings).

By the time he opened his office door, I was wondering how sharp-tongued Jane could have endured Bubba Sewell. When I saw that he had three employees in his smallish office, I realized he must be more intelligent than he seemed, and there were other unmistakable signs of prosperity—knick-knacks from the Sharper Image catalog, superior prints on the walls and leather upholstery on the chairs, and so on. I looked around Sewell's office while he gave some rapid instructions to the well-dressed red-haired secretary who was his first line of defense. She didn't seem like a fool, and she treated him with a kind of friendly respect.

"Well, well, now, let's see about you, Miss Teagarden," the lawyer said jovially when we were alone. "Where's that file? Gosh-a-Moses, it's somewhere in this mess here!"

Much rummaging among the papers on his desk. By now I was not deceived. Bubba Sewell for some reason found this Lord Peter Wimsey-like pretense of foolishness useful, but he was not foolish, not a bit.

"Here we are, it was right there all the time!" He flourished the file as though its existence had been in doubt.

I folded my hands in my lap and tried not to sigh obviously. I might have lots of time, but that didn't mean I wanted to spend it as an unwilling audience to a one-man performance.

"Hoo-wee, I'm sure glad you managed to turn it up," I said.

Bubba Sewell's hands stilled, and he shot me an extremely sharp look from under his bushy eyebrows.

"Miss Teagarden," he said, dropping his previous good-ole-boy manner completely, "Miss Engle left you everything."

THOSE ARE CERTAINLY some of the most thrilling words in the English language, but I wasn't going to let my jaw hit the floor. My hands, which had been clasped loosely in my lap, gripped convulsively for a minute, and I let out a long, silent breath.

"What's everything?" I asked.

Bubba Sewell told me that everything was Jane's house, its contents, and most of her bank account. She'd left her car and five thousand dollars to her cousin Parnell and his wife, Leah, on condition they took Madeleine the cat to live with them. I was relieved. I had never had a pet, and wouldn't have known what to do with the creature.

I had no idea what I should be saying or doing. I was so stunned I couldn't think what would be most seemly. I had done my mild grieving for Jane when I'd heard she'd gone, and at the graveside. I could tell that in a few minutes I was going to feel raw jubilation, since money problems had been troubling me. But at the moment mostly I was stunned.

"Why on earth did she do this?" I asked Bubba Sewell. "Do you know?"

"When she came in to make her will, last year when there was all that trouble with the club you two were in, she said that this was the best way she knew to make sure someone never forgot her. She didn't want her name up on a building somewhere. She wasn't a"—the lawyer searched for the right words—"philanthropist. Not a public person. She wanted to leave her money to an individual, not a cause, and I don't think she ever got along well with Parnell and Leah—do you know them?"

As a matter of fact, I am something rare in the South—a church hopper. I had met Jane's cousin and his wife at one of the churches I attended, I couldn't remember which one, though I thought it was one of Lawrenceton's more fundamentalist houses of worship. When they'd introduced themselves I'd asked if they were related to Jane, and Parnell had admitted he was a cousin, though with no great warmth. Leah had stared at me and said perhaps three words during the whole conversation.

"I've met them," I told Sewell.

"They're old and they haven't had any children," Sewell told me. "Jane felt they wouldn't outlast her long and would probably leave all her money to their church, which she didn't want. So she thought and thought and settled on you."

I thought and thought myself for a little bit. I looked up to find the lawyer eyeing me with speculation and some slight, impersonal disapproval. I figured he thought Jane should have left her money to cancer research or the SPCA or the orphanage.

"How much is in the account?" I asked briskly.

"Oh, in the checking account, maybe three thousand," he said. "I have the latest statements in this file. Of course, there are a few bills yet to come from Jane's last stay in the hospital, but her insurance will pick up most of that."

Three thousand! That was nice. I could finish paying for my car, which would help my monthly bill situation a lot.

"You said 'checking account,'" I said, after I'd thought for a moment. "Is there another account?"

"Oh, you bet," said Sewell, with a return of his former bonhomie. "Yes, ma'am! Miss Jane had a savings account she hardly ever touched. I tried a couple of times to interest her in investing it or at least buying a CD or a bond, but she said no, she liked her cash in her bank." Sewell shook his receding hairline several times over this and tilted back in his chair.

I had a vicious moment of hoping it would go all the way over with him in it.

"Could you please tell me how much is in the savings account?" I asked through teeth that were not quite clenched.

Bubba Sewell lit up. I had finally asked the right question. He catapulted forward in his chair to a mighty squeal of springs, pounced on the file, and extracted another bank statement.

"Wel-l-l-l," he drawled, puffing on the slit envelope and pulling out the paper inside, "as of last month, that account had in it—let's see—right, about five hundred and fifty thousand dollars."

Maybe this wasn't the worst year of my life after all.

TWO

I FLOATED OUT OF Bubba Sewell's office, trying not to look as gleeful as I felt. He walked with me to the elevator, looking down at me as if he couldn't figure me out. Well, it was mutual, but I wasn't caring right now, no sirree.

"She inherited it from her mother," Sewell said. "Most of it. Also, when her mother died, Miss Engle sold her mother's house, which was very large and brought a great price, and she split the money from that with her brother. Then her brother died and left her his nearly intact share of the house money, plus his estate, which she turned into cash. He was a banker in Atlanta."

I had money. I had a *lot* of money.

"I'll meet you at Jane's house tomorrow, and we'll have a look around at the contents, and I'll have a few things for you to sign. Would nine-thirty be convenient?"

I nodded with my lips pressed together so I wouldn't grin at him.

"And you know where it is?"

"Yes," I breathed, thankful the elevator had come at last and the doors were opening.

"Well, I'll see you tomorrow morning, Miss Teagarden," the lawyer said, setting his black glasses back on his nose and turning away as the doors closed with me inside.

I thought a scream of joy would echo up the elevator shaft, so I quietly but ecstatically said, "Heeheeheeheehee," all the way down and did a little jig before the doors opened on the marble lobby.

I MANAGED TO GET HOME to the town house on Parson Road without hitting another car, and pulled into my parking place planning how I could celebrate. The young married couple who'd taken Robin's town house, to the left of mine, waved back hesitantly in answer to my beaming hello. The Crandalls' parking space to the right was empty; they were visiting a married son in another town. The woman who'd finally rented Bankston Waite's town house was at work, as always. There was a strange car parked in the second space allotted to my apartment, but since I didn't see anyone I assumed it was a guest of one of the other tenants who didn't know how to read.

I opened my patio gate singing to myself and hopping around happily (I am not much of a dancer) and surprised a strange man in black sticking a note to my back door.

It was a toss-up as to which of us was the more startled.

It took me a moment of staring to figure out who the man was. I finally recognized him as the Episcopal priest who'd performed Mother's wedding and Jane Engle's funeral. I'd talked to him at the wedding reception, but not at this morning's funeral. He was a couple of inches over six feet, probably in his late thirties, with dark hair beginning to gray to the color of his eyes, a neat mustache, and a clerical collar.

"Miss Teagarden, I was just leaving you a note," he said, recovering neatly from his surprise at my singing, dancing entrance.

"Father Scott," I said firmly, his name popping into my head at the last second. "Good to see you."

"You seem happy today," he said, showing excellent teeth in a cautious smile. Maybe he thought I was drunk.

"Well, you know I was at Jane's funeral," I began, but when his eyebrows flew up I realized I'd started at the wrong end.

"Please come in, Father, and I'll tell you why I'm so cheerful when it might seem . . . inappropriate."

"Well, if you have a minute, I'll come in. Maybe I caught you at a bad time? And please call me Aubrey."

"No, this is fine. And call me Aurora. Or Roe, most people just call me Roe." Actually, I'd wanted a little alone time to get used to the idea of being rich, but telling someone would be fun too. I tried to remember how messy the place was. "Please come in, I'll make some coffee." And I just laughed.

He surely thought I was crazy as a loon, but he had to come in now.

"I haven't seen you to talk to since my mother got married," I babbled, as I twisted my key in the lock and flung open the door into the kitchen and living area. Good, it was quite neat.

"John's a wonderful man and a staunch member of the congregation," he said, having to look down at me quite sharply now that I was close. Why didn't I ever meet short men? I was doomed to go through life with a crick in my neck. "John and your mother are still on their honeymoon?"

"Yes, they're having such a good time I wouldn't be surprised if they stayed longer. My mother hasn't taken a vacation in at least six years. You know she owns a real estate business."

"That's what John told me," Aubrey Scott said politely. He was still standing right inside the door.

"Oh, I forgot my manners! Please come have a seat!" I tossed my purse on the counter and waved at the matching tan suede love seat and chair in the "living area," which lay beyond the "kitchen area."

The chair was clearly my special chair, from the brass lamp behind it for reading light to the small table loaded with my current book, a stained coffee mug, and a few magazines. Aubrey Scott wisely chose one end of the love seat.

"Listen," I said, perching opposite him on the edge of my chair, "I've got to tell you why I'm so giddy today. Normally I'm not like this at all." Which was true, more's the pity. "Jane Engle just left me a bunch of money, and, even though it may sound greedy, I've got to tell you I'm happy as a clam about it."

"I don't blame you," he said sincerely. I have noticed that, if there is one thing ministers are good at projecting, it is sincerity. "If someone had left me a bunch of money, I'd be dancing, too. I had no idea Jane was a—that Jane had a lot to leave anyone."

"Me either. She never lived like she had money. Let me get you a drink. Coffee? Or maybe a real drink?" I figured I could ask that, him being Episcopal. If he'd been, say, Parnell and Leah Engle's pastor, that question would have earned me a stiff lecture.

"If by real drink you mean one with alcohol, I wouldn't turn one down. It's after five o'clock, and conducting a funeral always drains me. What do you have? Any Seagram's, by any chance?"

"As a matter of fact, yes. What about a seven and seven?"

"Sounds great."

As I mixed the Seagram's 7 with the 7 Up, added ice, and even produced cocktail napkins and nuts, it finally struck me as odd that the Episcopal priest would come to call. I couldn't exactly say, "What are you doing here?" but I was curious. Well, he'd get around to it. Most of the preachers in Lawrenceton had had a go at roping me in at one time or another. I am a fairly regular churchgoer, but I seldom go to the same church twice in a row.

It would have been nice to run upstairs to change from my hot black funeral dress to something less formal, but I figured he would run out the back door if I proposed to slip into something comfortable.

I did take off my heels, caked with mud from the cemetery, after I sat down.

"So tell me about your inheritance," he suggested after an awkward pause.

I couldn't recapture my initial excitement, but I could feel a grin turning up my lips as I told him about my friendship with Jane Engle and Bubba Sewell's approach after the service was over.

"That's amazing," he murmured. "You've been blessed."

"Yes, I have," I agreed wholeheartedly.

"And you say you weren't a particular friend of Jane's?"

"No. We were friends, but at times a month would go by without our seeing each other. And not thinking anything about it, either."

"I don't suppose you've had enough time to plan anything to do with this unexpected legacy."

"No." And if he suggested some worthy cause, I would really resent it. I just wanted to be in proud ownership of a little house and a big (to me, anyway) fortune, at least for a while.

"I'm glad for you," he said, and there was another awkward pause.

"Was there anything I could do to help you, did your note say?..." I trailed off. I tried to manage a look of intelligent expectancy.

"Well," he said with an embarrassed laugh, "actually, I...this is so stupid, I'm acting like I was in high school again. Actually... I just wanted to ask you out. On a date."

"A date," I repeated blankly.

I saw instantly that my astonishment was hurting him.

"No, it's not that that's peculiar," I said hastily. "I just wasn't expecting it."

"Because I'm a minister."

"Well—yes."

He heaved a sigh and opened his mouth with a resigned expression.

"No, no!" I said, throwing my hands up. "Don't make an 'I'm only human' speech, if you were going to! I was gauche, I admit it! Of course I'll go out with you!"

I felt like I owed it to him now.

"You're not involved in another relationship at the moment?" he asked carefully.

I wondered if he had to wear the collar on dates.

"No, not for a while. In fact, I went to the wedding of my last relationship a few months ago."

Suddenly Aubrey Scott smiled, and his big gray eyes crinkled up at the corners, and he looked good enough to eat.

"What would you like to do? The movies?"

I hadn't had a date since Arthur and I had split. Anything sounded good to me.

"Okay," I said.

"Maybe we can go to the early show and go out to eat afterward."

"Fine. When?"

"Tomorrow night?"

"Okay. The early show usually starts at five if we go to the triplex. Anything special you want to see?"

"Let's get there and decide."

There could easily be three movies I did not want to see showing at one time, but the chances were at least one of them would be tolerable.

"Okay," I said again. "But if you're taking me out to supper, I want to treat you to the movie."

He looked doubtful. "I'm kind of a traditional guy," he said. "But if you want to do it that way, that'll be a new experience for me." He sounded rather courageous about it.

After he left, I slowly finished my drink. I wondered if the rules for dating clergymen were different from the rules for dating regular guys. I told myself sternly that clergymen *are* regular guys, just regular guys who professionally relate to God. I knew I was being naive in thinking I had to act differently with Aubrey Scott than I would with another date. If I was so malicious or off-color or just plain wrongheaded that I had to constantly censor my conversation with a minister, then I needed the experience anyway. Perhaps it would be like dating a psychiatrist; you would always worry about what he spotted about you that you didn't know. Well, this date would be a "learning experience" for me.

What a day! I shook my head as I plodded up the stairs to my bedroom. From being a poor, worried, spurned librarian I'd become a wealthy, secure, datable heiress.

The impulse to share my new status was almost irresistible. But Amina was back in Houston and preoccupied by her upcoming marriage, my mother was on her honeymoon (boy, would I enjoy telling *her*), my co-worker Lillian Schmidt would find some way to make me feel guilty about it, and my sort-of-friend Sally Allison would want to put it in the paper. I'd really like to tell Robin Crusoe, my mystery writer friend, but he was in the big city of Atlanta, having decided the commute from Lawrenceton to his teaching position there was too much to handle—or at least that was the reason he'd given me. Unless I could tell him face-to-face, I wouldn't enjoy it. His face was one of my favorites.

Maybe some celebrations are just meant to be private. A big wahoo would have been out of line anyway, since Jane had had to die in order for this celebration to be held. I took off the black dress and put on a bathrobe and went downstairs to watch an old movie and eat half a bag of pretzels and then half a quart of chocolate fudge ripple ice cream.

Heiresses can do anything.

IT WAS RAINING the next morning, a short summer shower that promised a steamy afternoon. The thunderclaps were sharp and scary, and I found myself jumping at each one as I drank my coffee. After I retrieved the paper (only a little wet) from the otherwise unused front doorstep that faced Parson Road, it began to slow down. By the time I'd had my shower and was dressed and ready for my appointment with Bubba Sewell, the sun had

come out and mist began to rise from the puddles
in the parking lot beyond the patio. I watched CNN
for a while—heiresses need to be well-informed—
fidgeted with my makeup, ate a banana, and
scrubbed the kitchen sink, and then finally it was
time to go.

I couldn't figure out why I was so excited. The
money wasn't going to be piled in the middle of the
floor. I'd have to wait roughly two months to actually be able to spend it, Sewell had said. I'd been
in Jane's little house before, and there was nothing
so special about it.

Of course, now I owned it. I'd never owned
something that big before.

I was independent of my mother, too. I could've
made it by myself on my librarian's salary, though
it would have been hard, but having the resident
manager's job and therefore a free place to live and
a little extra salary had certainly made a big difference.

I'd woken several times during the night and
thought about living in Jane's house. My house. Or
after probate I could sell it and buy elsewhere.

That morning, starting up my car to drive to
Honor Street, the world was so full of possibilities
it was just plain terrifying, in a happy roller-coaster
way.

Jane's house was in one of the older residential
neighborhoods. The streets were named for vir-

tues. One reached Honor by way of Faith. Honor was a dead end, and Jane's house was the second from the corner on the right side. The houses in this neighborhood tended to be small—two or three bedrooms—with meticulously kept little yards dominated by large trees circled with flower beds. Jane's front yard was half filled by a live oak on the right side that shaded the bay window in the living room. The driveway ran in on the left, and there was a deep single-car carport attached to the house. A door in the rear of the carport told me there was some kind of storage room there. The kitchen door opened onto the carport, or you could (as I'd done as a visitor) park in the driveway and take the curving sidewalk to the front door. The house was white, like all the others on the street, and there were azalea bushes planted all around the foundation; it would be lovely in spring.

The marigolds Jane had planted around her mailbox had died from lack of water, I saw as I got out of the car. Somehow that little detail sobered me up completely. The hands that had planted those withered yellow flowers were now six feet underground and idle forever.

I was a bit early, so I took the time to look around at my new neighborhood. The corner house, to the right of Jane's as I faced it, had beautiful big climbing rosebushes round the front porch. The one to the left had had a lot added on, so that the original simple lines of the house were obscured. It had been bricked in, a garage with an apartment on top had been connected to the house by a roofed walk, a deck had been tacked on the back. The result was not happy. The last house on the street was next to that, and I remembered that the newspaper editor, Macon Turner, who had once dated my mother, lived there. The house directly across the street from Jane's, a pretty little house with canary yellow shutters, had a realtor's sign up with a big red SOLD slapped across it. The corner house on that side of the street was the one Melanie Clark, another member of the defunct Real Murders club, had rented for a while: now a Big Wheel parked in the driveway indicated children on the premises. One house took up the last two lots on that side, a rather dilapidated place with only one tree in a large yard. It sat blankfaced, the yellowing shades pulled down. A wheelchair ramp had been built on.

At this hour on a summer morning, the quiet was peaceful. But, behind the houses on Jane's side of the street, there was the large parking lot for the junior high school, with the school's own high fence keeping trash from being pitched in Jane's yard and students from using it as a shortcut. I was sure there would be more noise during the school year, but now that parking lot sat empty. By and by, a woman from the corner house on the other side of the street started up a lawn mower and that wonderful summer sound made me feel relaxed.

You planned for this, Jane, I thought. You wanted me to go in your house. You know me and you picked me for this.

Bubba Sewell's BMW pulled up to the curb, and I took a deep breath and walked toward it.

HE HANDED ME THE KEYS. My hand closed over them. It felt like a formal investiture. "There's no problem with you going on and working in this house now, clearing it out or preparing it for sale or whatever you want to do, it belongs to you and no one says different. I've advertised for anyone with claims on the estate to come forward, and so far no one has. But of course we can't spend any of the money," he admonished me with a wagging finger. "The house bills are still coming to me as executor, and they will until probate is settled."

This was like being a week away from your birthday when you were six.

"This one," he said, pointing to one key, "opens the dead bolt on the front door. This one opens the punch lock on the front door. This little one is to Jane's safe deposit box at Eastern National, there's a little jewelry and a few papers in it, nothing much."

I unlocked the door and we stepped in.

"Shit," said Bubba Sewell in an unlawyerly way.

There was a heap of cushions from the living room chairs thrown around. I could look through the living room into the kitchen and see similar disorder there.

Someone had broken in.

ONE OF THE REAR WINDOWS, the one in the back bedroom, had been broken. It had been a pristine little room with chaste twin beds covered in white chenille. The wallpaper was floral and unobtrusive, and the glass was easy to sweep up on the hardwood floor. The first things I found in my new house were the dustpan and the broom, lying on the floor by the tall broom closet in the kitchen.

"I don't think anything's gone," Sewell said with a good deal of surprise, "but I'll call the police anyway. These people, they read the obituaries in the paper and go around breaking into the houses that are empty."

I stood holding a dustpan full of glass. "So why isn't anything missing?" I asked. "The TV is still in the living room. The clock-radio is still in here, and there's a microwave in the kitchen."

"Maybe you're just plain lucky," Sewell said, his eyes resting on me thoughtfully. He polished his glasses on a gleaming white handkerchief. "Or maybe the kids were so young that just breaking in was enough thrill. Maybe they got scared halfway through. Who knows."

"Tell me a few things." I sat on one of the white beds and he sat down opposite me. The broken window (the storm this morning had soaked the curtains) made the room anything but intimate. I propped the broom against my knee and put the dustpan on the floor. "What happened with this house after Jane died? Who came in here? Who has keys?"

"Jane died in the hospital, of course," Sewell began. "When she first went in, she still thought she might come home, so she had me hire a maid to come in and clean . . . empty the garbage, clear the perishables out of the refrigerator, and so on. Jane's neighbor to the side, Torrance Rideout—you know him?—he offered to keep her yard mowed for her, so he has a key to the tool and storage room, that's the door at the back of the carport."

I nodded.

"But that's the only key he had," the lawyer said, getting back on target. "Then a few days later, when Jane learned—she wasn't coming home . . ."

"I visited her in the hospital, and she never said a word to me," I murmured.

"She didn't like to talk about it. What was there to say? she asked me. I think she was right. But anyway . . . I kept the electricity and gas—the heat is gas, everything else is electric—hooked up, but I came over here and unplugged everything but the freezer—it's in the toolroom and it has food in it—

and I stopped the papers and started having Jane's mail kept at the post office, then I'd pick it up and take it to her, it wasn't any trouble to me, my mail goes to the post office, too..."

Sewell had taken care of everything for Jane. Was this the care of a lawyer for a good client or the devotion of a friend?

"So," he was saying briskly, "the little bitty operating expenses for this house will come out of the estate, but I trust you won't mind, we kept it at a minimum. You know when you completely turn off the air or heat into a house, the house just seems to go downhill almost immediately, and there was always the slight chance Jane might make it and come home."

"No, of course I don't mind paying the electric bill. Do Parnell and Leah have a key?"

"No, Jane was firm about that. Parnell came to me and offered to go through and get Jane's clothes and things packed away, but of course I told him no."

"Oh?"

"They're yours," he said simply. "Everything"—and he gave that some emphasis, or was it only my imagination—"everything in this house is yours. Parnell and Leah know about their five thousand, and Jane herself handed him the keys to her car two days before she died and let him take it from this carport, but, other than that, *whatever* is in this house''—and suddenly I was alert and very nearly scared—''is yours to deal with however you see fit.''

My eyes narrowed with concentration. What was he saying that he wasn't really saying?

Somewhere, somewhere in this house, lurked a problem. For some reason, Jane's legacy wasn't entirely benevolent. After calling the police about the break-in and calling the glass people to come to fix the window, Bubba Sewell took his departure.

''I don't think the police will even show up here since I couldn't tell them anything was missing. I'll stop by the station on my way back to the office, though.'' he said on his way out the door.

I was relieved to hear that. I'd met most of the local policemen when I dated Arthur; policemen really stick together. ''There's no point in turning on the air conditioner until that back bedroom window is fixed,'' Sewell added, ''but the thermostat is in the hall, when you need it.''

He was being mighty chary with my money. Now that I was so rich, I could fling open the windows and doors and set the thermostat on forty, if I wanted to do something so foolish and wasteful.

''If you have any problems, run into anything you can't handle, you just call me,'' Sewell said again. He'd expressed that sentiment several times, in several different ways. But just once he had said, ''Miss Jane had a high opinion of you, that you could tackle any problem that came your way and make a success of it."

I got the picture. By now I was so apprehensive, I heartily wanted Sewell to leave. Finally he was out the front door, and I knelt on the window seat in the bay window and partially opened the sectioned blinds surrounding it to watch his car pull away. When I was sure he was gone, I opened all the blinds and turned around to survey my new territory. The living room was carpeted, the only room in the house that was, and when Jane had had this done she'd run the carpet right up onto the window seat so that it was seamlessly covered, side, top, and all. There were some hand-embroidered pillows arranged on it, and the effect was very pretty. The carpet Jane had been so partial to was a muted rose with a tiny blue pattern, and her living room furniture (a sofa and two armchairs) picked up that shade of blue, while the lamp shades were white or rose. There was a small color television arranged for easy viewing from Jane's favorite chair. The antique table beside that chair was still stacked with magazines, a strange assortment that summed up Jane—*Southern Living, Mystery Scene, Lear's,* and a publication from the church.

The walls of this small room were lined with freestanding shelves overflowing with books. My mouth watered when I looked at them. One thing I knew Jane and I had shared: we loved books, we especially loved mysteries, and more than anything we loved books about real murders. Jane's collection had always been my envy.

At the rear of the living room was a dining area, with a beautiful table and chairs I believed Jane had inherited from her mother. I knew nothing about antiques and cared less, but the table and chairs were gleaming under a light coating of dust, and, as I straightened the cushions and pushed the couch back to its place against the wall (why would anyone move a couch when he broke into a house?), I was already worried about caring for the set.

At least all the books hadn't been thrown on the floor. Straightening this room actually took only a few moments.

I moved into the kitchen. I was avoiding Jane's bedroom. It could wait.

The kitchen had a large double window that looked onto the backyard, and a tiny table with two chairs was set right in front of the window. Here was where Jane and I had had coffee when I'd visited her, if she hadn't taken me into the living room.

The disorder in the kitchen was just as puzzling. The shallow upper cabinets were fine, had not been touched, but the deeper bottom cabinets had been emptied carelessly. Nothing had been poured out of its container or wantonly vandalized, but the contents had been moved as though the cabinet itself were the object of the search, not possible loot that

could be taken away. And the broom closet, tall and
thin, had received special attention. I flipped on the
kitchen light and stared at the wall in the back of
the closet. It was marred with "... knife gouges,
sure as shooting," I mumbled. While I stooped to
reload the cabinet shelves with pots and pans, I
thought about those gouges. The breaker-in had
wanted to see if there was something fake about the
back of the closet; that was the only interpretation
I could put on the holes. And only the large bottom cabinets had been disturbed; only the large
pieces of furniture in the living room.

So, Miss Genius, he was looking for something
large. Okay, "he" could be a woman, but I wasn't
going to the trouble of thinking "he or she." "He"
would do very well for now. What large thing could
Jane Engle have concealed in her house that anyone could possibly want enough to break in for?
Unanswerable until I knew more, and I definitely
had the feeling I would know more.

I finished picking up the kitchen and returned to
the guest bedroom. The only disturbance there,
now I'd cleared up the glass, was to the two single
closets, which had been opened and emptied. There
again, no attempt had been made to destroy or
mutilate the items that had been taken from the
closets; they'd just been emptied swiftly and thoroughly. Jane had stored her luggage in one closet,
and the larger suitcases had been opened. Out-of-

season clothes, boxes of pictures and mementos, a portable sewing machine, two boxes of Christmas decorations...all things I had to check through and decide on, but for now it was enough to shovel them all back in. As I hung up a heavy coat, I noticed the walls in these closets had been treated the same way as the broom closet in the kitchen.

The attic stairs pulled down in the little hall that had a bedroom door at each end and the bathroom door in the middle. A broad archway led from this hall back into the living room. This house actually was smaller than my town house by quite a few square feet, I realized. If I moved I would have less room but more independence.

It was going to be hot up in the attic, but it would certainly be much hotter by the afternoon. I gripped the cord and pulled down. I unfolded the stairs and stared at them doubtfully. They didn't look any too sturdy.

Jane hadn't liked to use them either, I found, after I'd eased my way up the creaking wooden stairs. There was very little in the attic but dust and disturbed insulation; the searcher had been up here, too, and an itchy time he must have had of it. A leftover strip of the living room carpet had been unrolled, a chest had its drawers halfway pulled out. I closed up the attic with some relief and washed my dusty hands and face in the bathroom sink. The bathroom was a good size, with a large

linen cabinet below which was a half door that
opened onto a wide space suitable for a laundry
basket to hold dirty clothes. This half closet had
received the same attention as the ones in the
kitchen and guest bedroom.

The searcher was trying to find a secret hiding
place for something that could be put in a drawer
but not hidden behind books... something that
couldn't be hidden between sheets and towels but
could be hidden in a large pot. I tried to image Jane
hiding—a suitcase full of money? What else? A box
of—documents revealing a terrible secret? I opened
the top half of the closet to look at Jane's neatly
folded sheets and towels without actually seeing
them. I should be grateful those hadn't been
dumped out, too, I mused with half of my brain,
since Jane had been a champion folder; the towels
were neater than I'd ever get them, and the sheets
appeared to have been ironed, something I hadn't
seen since I was a child.

Not money or documents; those could have been
divided to fit into the spaces that the searcher had
ignored.

The door bell rang, making me jump a foot.

It was only the glass repair people, a husband
and wife team I'd called when window problems
arose at my mother's apartments. They accepted
me being at this address without any questions, and
the woman commented when she saw the back

window that lots of houses were getting broken into these days, though it had been a rarity when she'd been "a kid."

"Those people coming out from the city," she told me seriously, raising her heavily penciled eyebrows.

"Reckon so?" I asked, to establish my goodwill.

"Oh sure, honey. They come out here to get away from the city, but they bring their city habits with 'em."

Lawrenceton loved the commuters' money without actually trusting or loving the commuters.

While they tackled removing the broken glass and replacing it, I went into Jane's front bedroom. Somehow entering it was easier with someone else in the house. I am not superstitious, at least not consciously, but it seemed to me that Jane's presence was strongest in her bedroom, and having people busy in another room in the house made my entering her room less...personal.

It was a large bedroom, and Jane had a queen-sized four-poster with one bed table, a substantial chest of drawers, and a vanity table with a large mirror comfortably arranged. In the now-familiar way, the double closet was open and the contents tossed out simply to get them out of the way. There were built-in shelves on either side of the closet, and the shoes and purses had been swept from these, too.

There's not much as depressing as someone else's old shoes, when you have the job of disposing of them. Jane had not cared to put her money into her clothes and personal accessories. I could not ever recall Jane wearing anything I noticed particularly, or even anything I could definitely say was brand new. Her shoes were not expensive and were all well-worn. It seemed to me Jane had not enjoyed her money at all; she'd lived in her little house with her Penney's and Sears wardrobe, buying books as her only extravagance. And she'd always struck me as content; she'd worked until she'd had to retire, and then come back to substitute at the library. Somehow this all seemed melancholy, and I had to shake myself to pull out of the blues.

What I needed, I told myself briskly, was to return with some large cartons, pack all Jane's clothing away, and haul the cartons over to the Goodwill. Jane had been a little taller than I, and thicker, too; nothing would fit or be suitable. I piled all the flung-down clothes and tossed the shoes on the bed; no point in loading them back into the closet when I knew I didn't need or want them. When that was done, I spent a few minutes pressing and poking and tapping in the closet myself.

It just sounded and felt like a closet to me.

I gave up and perched on the end of the bed, thinking of all the pots and pans, towels and sheets, magazines and books, sewing kits and Christmas ornaments, bobby pins and hair nets, handkerchiefs, that were now mine and my responsibility to do something with. Just thinking of it was tiring. I listened idly to the voices of the couple working in the back bedroom. You would have thought that since they lived together twenty-four hours a day they would've said all they could think of to say, but I could hear one offer the other a comment every now and then. This calm, intermittent dialogue seemed companionable, and I went into kind of a trance sitting on the end of that bed.

I had to be at work that afternoon for three hours, from one to four. I'd have just time to get home and get ready for my date with Aubrey Scott . . . did I really need to shower and change before we went to the movies? After going up in the attic, it would be a good idea. Today was much hotter than yesterday. Cartons . . . where to get some sturdy ones? Maybe the Dumpster behind Wal-Mart? The liquor store had good cartons, but they were too small for clothes packing. Would Jane's bookshelves look okay standing by my bookshelves? Should I move my books here? I could make the guest bedroom into a study. The only person I'd ever had as an overnight guest who didn't actually sleep with me, my half brother Phillip, lived out in California now.

"We're through, Miss Teagarden," called the husband half of the team.

I shook myself out of my stupor.

"Send the bill to Bubba Sewell in the Jasper Building. Here's the address," and I ripped a piece of paper off a tablet Jane had left by the telephone. The telephone! Was it hooked up? No, I found after the repair team had left. Sewell had deemed it an unnecessary expense. Should I have it hooked back up? Under what name? Would I have two phone numbers, one here and one at the town house?

I'd had my fill of my inheritance for one day. Just as I locked the front door, I heard footsteps rustling through the grass and turned to see a barrel-chested man of about forty-five coming from the house to my left.

"Hi," he said quickly. "You're our new neighbor, I take it."

"You must be Torrance Rideout. Thanks for taking such good care of the lawn."

"Well, that's what I wanted to ask about." Close up, Torrance Rideout looked like a man who'd once been handsome and still wasn't without the old sex appeal. His hair was muddy brown and only a few flecks of gray, and he looked like his beard would be heavy enough to shave twice a day. He had a craggy face, brown eyes surrounded by what I thought of as sun wrinkles, a dark tan, and he was wearing a green golf shirt and navy shorts. "My wife, Marcia, and I were real sorry about Jane. She was a real good neighbor and we were sure sorry about her passing."

I didn't feel like I was the right person to accept condolences, but I wasn't about to explain I'd inherited Jane's house not because we were the best of friends but because Jane wanted someone who could remember her for a good long while. So I just nodded, and hoped that would do.

Torrance Rideout seemed to accept that. "Well, I've been mowing the yard, and I was wondering if you wanted me to do it one more week until you get your own yardman or mow it yourself, or just whatever you want to do. I'll be glad to do it."

"You've already been to so much trouble..."

"Nope, no trouble. I told Jane when she went in the hospital not to worry about the yard, I'd take care of it. I've got a riding mower, I just ride it on over when I do my yard, and there ain't that much weed eating to do, just around a couple of flower beds. I did get Jane's mower out to do the tight places the riding mower can't get. But what I did want to tell you, someone dug a little in the back-yard."

We'd walked over to my car while Torrance talked, and I'd pulled out my keys. Now I stopped with my fingers on the car door handle. "Dug up the backyard?" I echoed incredulously. Come to think of it, that wasn't so surprising. I thought about it for a moment. Okay, something that could be kept in a hole in the ground as well as hidden in a house.

"I filled the holes back in," Torrance went on, "and Marcia's been keeping a special lookout since she's home during the day."

I told Torrance someone had entered the house, and he expressed the expected astonishment and disgust. He hadn't seen the broken window when he'd last mowed the backyard two days before, he told me.

"I do thank you," I said again. "You've done so much."

"No, no," he protested quickly. "We were kind of wondering if you were going to put the house on the market, or live in it yourself....Jane was our neighbor for so long, we kind of worry about breaking in a new one!"

"I haven't made up my mind," I said, and left it at that, which seemed to stump Torrance Rideout.

"Well, see, we rent out that room over our garage," he explained, "and we have for a good long while. This area is not exactly zoned for rental units, but Jane never minded and our neighbor on the other side, Macon Turner, runs the paper, you know him? Macon never has cared. But new people in Jane's house, well, we didn't know..."

"I'll tell you the minute I make up my mind," I said in as agreeable a way as I could.

"Well, well. We appreciate it, and if you need anything, just come ask me or Marcia. I'm out of town off and on most weeks, selling office supplies believe it or not, but then I'm home every weekend and some afternoons, and, like I said, Marcia's home and she'd love to help if she could."

"Thank you for offering," I said. "And I'm sure I'll be talking to you soon. Thanks for all you've done with the yard."

And finally I got to leave. I stopped at Burger King for lunch, regretting that I hadn't grabbed one of Jane's books to read while I ate. But I had plenty to think about: the emptied closets, the holes in the backyard, the hint Bubba Sewell had given me that Jane had left me a problem to solve. The sheer physical task of clearing the house of what I didn't want, and then the decision about what to do with the house itself. At least all these thoughts were preferable to thinking of myself yet again as the jilted lover, brooding over the upcoming Smith baby... feeling somehow cheated by Lynn's pregnancy. It was much nicer to have decisions within my power to make, instead of having them made for me.

Now! I told myself briskly, to ward off the melancholy, as I dumped my cup and wrapper in the trash bin and left the restaurant. Now to work, then home, then out on a real date, and tomorrow get out early in the morning to find those boxes!

I should have remembered that my plans seldom work out.

THREE

WORK THAT AFTERNOON more or less drifted by. I was on the checkout/check-in desk for three hours, making idle conversation with the patrons. I knew most of them by name, and had known them all my life. I could have made their day by telling each and every one of them, including my fellow librarians, about my good fortune, but somehow it seemed immodest. And it wasn't like my mother had died, which would have been an understandable transfer of fortune. Jane's legacy, which was beginning to make me (almost) more anxious than glad, was so inexplicable that it embarrassed me to talk about it. Everyone would find out about it sooner or later...mentioning it now would be much more understandable than keeping silent. The other librarians were talking about Jane anyway; she had substituted here after her retirement from the school system and had been a great reader for years. I'd seen several of my co-workers at the funeral.

But I couldn't think of any casual way to drop Jane's legacy into the conversation. I could already picture the eyebrows flying up, the looks that would pass when my back was turned. In ways not yet realized, Jane had made my life much easier. In ways I was just beginning to perceive, Jane had made my life extremely complicated. I decided, in the end, just to keep my mouth shut and take what the local gossip mill had to dish out.

Lillian Schmidt almost shook my resolution when she observed that she'd seen Bubba Sewell, the lawyer, call to me at the cemetery.

"What did he want?" Lillian asked directly, as she pulled the front of her blouse together to make the gap between the buttons temporarily disappear.

I just smiled.

"Oh! Well, he is single—*now*—but you know Bubba's been married twice," she told me with relish. The buttons were already straining again.

"Who to?" I asked ungrammatically, to steer her off my own conversation with the lawyer.

"First to Carey Osland. I don't know if you know her, she lives right by Jane . . . you remember what happened to Carey later on, her second husband? Mike Osland? Went out for diapers one night right after Carey'd had that little girl, and never came back? Carey had them search everywhere for that man, she just could not believe he would walk out on her like that, but he must have."

"But before Mike Osland, Carey was married to Bubba Sewell?"

"Oh, right. Yes, for a little while, no children. Then after a year, Bubba married some girl from Atlanta, her daddy was some big lawyer, everyone thought it would be a good thing for his career." Lillian did not bother to remember the name since the girl was not a Lawrenceton native and the marriage had not lasted. "But that didn't work out, she cheated on him."

I made vague regretful noises so that Lillian would continue.

"Then—hope you enjoy these, Miz Darwell, have a nice day—he started dating your friend Lizanne Buckley."

"He's dating Lizanne?" I said in some surprise. "I haven't seen her in quite a while. I've been mailing in my bill instead of taking it by, like I used to."

Lizanne was the receptionist at the utility company. Lizanne was beautiful and agreeable, slow-witted but sure, like honey making its inexorable progress across a buttered pancake. Her parents had died the year before, and for a while that had put a crease across the perfect forehead and tear marks down the magnolia white cheeks, but gradually Lizanne's precious routine had encompassed this terrible change in her life and she had willed herself to forget the awfulness of it. She had sold her parents' house, bought herself one just like it with the proceeds, and resumed breaking hearts.

Bubba Sewell must have been an optimist and a man who worshiped beauty to date the notoriously untouchable Lizanne. I wouldn't have thought it of him.

"So maybe he and Lizanne have broken up, he wants to take you out?" Lillian always got back on the track eventually.

"No, I'm going out with Aubrey Scott tonight," I said, having thought of this evasion during her recital of Bubba Sewell's marital woes. "The Episcopal priest. We met at my mother's wedding."

It worked, and Lillian's high pleasure at knowing this exclusive fact put her in a good humor the rest of the afternoon. I didn't realize how many Episcopalians there were in Lawrenceton until I went out with their priest.

Waiting in line for the movies I met at least five members of Aubrey's congregation. I tried to radiate respectability and wholesomeness, and kept wishing my wavy bunch of hair had been more cooperative when I'd tried to tame it before he picked me up. It flew in a warm cloud around my head, and for the hundredth time I thought of having it all cut off. At least my navy slacks and bright yellow shirt were neat and new, and my plain gold chain and earrings were good but—plain. Aubrey was in mufti, which definitely helped me to relax. He was disconcertingly attractive in his jeans and shirt; I had some definitely secular thoughts.

The movie we picked was a comedy, and we laughed at the same places, which was heartening. Our compatibility extended through dinner, where a mention of my mother's wedding prompted some reminiscences from Aubrey about weddings that had gone disastrously wrong. "And the flower girl threw up at my own wedding," he concluded.

"You've been married?" I said brilliantly. But he'd brought it up on purpose, of course, so I was doing the right thing.

"I'm a widower. She died three years ago of cancer," he said simply.

I looked at my plate real hard.

"I haven't dated too much since then," he went on. "I feel like I'm pretty—inept at it."

"You're doing fine so far," I told him.

He smiled, and it was a very attractive smile.

"From what the teenagers in my congregation tell me, dating's changed a lot in the last twenty years, since last I went out on a date. I don't want— I just want to clear the air. You seem a little nervous from time to time about being out with a minister."

"Well—yes."

"Okay. I'm not perfect, and I don't expect you to be perfect. Everyone has attitudes and opinions that are not exactly toeing the line spiritually; we're all trying, and it'll take our whole lives to get there. That's what I believe. I also don't believe in premarital sex; I'm waiting for something to change my mind on that issue, but so far it hasn't happened. Did you want to know any of that?''

"As a matter of fact, yes. That's just about exactly what I did want to know." What surprised me was the amount of relief I felt at the certainty that Aubrey would not try to get me to go to bed with him. Most dates I'd had in the past ten years, I'd spent half the time worried about what would happen when the guy took me home. Especially now, after my passionate involvement with Arthur, it was a load off my mind that Aubrey wouldn't expect me to make a decision about whether or not to go to bed with him. I brightened up and really began to enjoy myself. He didn't discuss his wife again, and I knew I would not introduce the subject.

Aubrey's ban on premarital sex did not include a ban on premarital kissing, I discovered when he walked me to my back door.

"Maybe we can go out again?"

"Give me a call," I said with a smile.

"Thanks for this evening."

"Thank *you*."

We parted with mutual goodwill, and as I scrubbed my face and pulled on my nightgown the next day didn't seem so daunting. I wasn't scheduled to work at the library, so I could work at Jane's house. My house. I couldn't get used to the ownership.

But thinking of the house led to worrying about the break-in, about the holes in the backyard I hadn't yet seen, about the object of this strange search. It must be an object too big to be in the safe deposit box Bubba Sewell had mentioned; besides, he had told me there was nothing much in the box, implying he had seen the contents already.

I drifted off to sleep thinking, Something that couldn't be divided, something that couldn't be flattened . . .

When I woke up in the morning I knew where that something must be hidden.

I FELT LIKE I WAS on a secret mission. After I scrambled into some jeans and a T-shirt and ate some toast, I checked the sketchy contents of my tool drawer. I wasn't sure what I would need. Probably Jane had these same basic things, but I didn't feel like rummaging around until I found them. I ended up with a claw hammer and two screwdrivers, and after a little thought I added a broad-bladed putty knife. I managed to stuff all these in my purse except the hammer, and finally I managed that; but the haft stuck up from the drawstringed gather. That wouldn't be too obvious, I told myself. I brushed my teeth hastily but didn't bother with makeup, so before eight o'clock I was pulling into the driveway on Honor.

I brought the car right up into the carport and entered through the kitchen door. The house was silent and stuffy. I found the thermostat in the little hall and pushed the switch to "cool." The central air hummed into life. I glanced through the rooms hastily; nothing seemed to have been disturbed during the night. I was sweating a little, and my hair kept sticking to my face, so I did track down a rubber band and pull it all back on my neck. I blew out a deep breath, braced my shoulders, and marched into the living room. I raised the blinds around the window seat to get as much light as possible, took out my tools, and began.

Whatever it was, it was in the window seat.

Jane had had it carpeted over, so no one would think of it as a container, but only as a feature of the room, a nice place to put a plant or some pretty pillows or a flower arrangement. The installer had done a good job, and I had a hell of a time prizing up the carpet. I saw Torrance Rideout pull out of his driveway, glance at the house, and drive away to work. A pretty, plump woman walked a fat dachshund down to the end of the street and back, letting the dog perform on my yard, I noticed indignantly. I recognized her, after I thought of it awhile, as I pried and pulled at the rose-colored carpet with its little blue figure. She was Carey Osland, once married to Bubba Sewell, once married to Mike Osland, the man who had decamped in such a spectacularly callous way. Carey Osland must live in the corner house with the big climbing roses by the front porch.

I plugged away, trying not to speculate about what was in the window seat, and finally I loosened enough carpet to grab an edge with both hands and yank.

The bay window really did contain a window seat with a hinged lid. I had been right. So why didn't I feel triumphant?

Whatever was in the house was my problem, Bubba Sewell had said.

Taking a deep breath, I raised the lid and peered into the window seat. The sun streamed down into the seat, bathing its contents with a gentle morning glow. There was a rather yellow pillowcase inside, a pillowcase with something round in it.

I reached in and pulled at the corner of the pillowcase, gingerly working it back and forth, trying not to disturb its contents. But finally I had to pull it off altogether, and the thing that had been in the pillowcase rolled onto its side.

A skull grinned up at me.

"Oh my God," I said, slamming the lid down and sitting on the seat, covering my face with both trembling hands. The next minute I was in frantic action, lowering those blinds and shutting them, checking to make sure the front door was locked, finding the light switch, and flipping on the overhead light in the suddenly darkened room.

I opened the window seat again, hoping its contents had miraculously changed.

The skull still lay there with its slack-jawed grin.

Then the doorbell rang.

I jumped and squeaked. For a moment I stood indecisively. Then I tossed the tools into the seat with the thing, shut the lid, and yanked the loose carpet back up. It wouldn't settle back into place very well, having been removed so inexpertly, but I did the best I could and then heaped the fancy pillows around the edges to conceal the damage. But the carpet still sagged a little. I pushed it into place, weighted it down with my purse. It still pouched. I grabbed some books from the shelves and stacked them on the window seat, too. Much better. The carpet stayed in place. The doorbell rang again. I stood for a moment composing my face.

Carey Osland, minus the dachshund, smiled at me in a friendly way when I finally opened the door. Her dark chestnut hair was lightly threaded with gray, but her round, pretty face was unlined. She was wearing a dress that was one step up from a bathrobe, and scuffed loafers.

"Hi, neighbor," she said cheerfully. "Aurora Teagarden, isn't it?"

"Yes," I said, making a huge effort to sound casual and calm.

"I'm Carey Osland, I live in the house with the roses, on the corner," and she pointed.

"I remember meeting you before, Carey, at a bridal shower, I think."

"That's right—a long time ago. Whose was it?"

"Come in, come on in.... Wasn't it Amina's shower, after she eloped?"

"Well, it must have been, 'cause that was when I was working at her mother's dress shop, that's why I got invited. I work at Marcus Hatfield now."

Marcus Hatfield was the Lord & Taylor of Lawrenceton.

"That's why I'm such a slob now," Carey went on smilingly. "I get so tired of being dressed up."

"Your nails look great," I said admiringly. I am always impressed by someone who can wear long nails and keep them polished. I was also trying very hard not to think about the window seat, not to even glance in that direction. I had waved Carey to the couch so she'd have her back partially to it when she half-turned to talk to me as I sat in the armchair.

"Oh, honey, they're not real," Carey said warmly. "I never could keep my nails from chipping and getting broken.... So, you and Jane must have been good friends?"

The unexpected change of subject and Carey's very understandable curiosity took me by surprise.

My neighbors were definitely not of the big city impersonal variety.

"She left me the house," I stated, figuring that settled that.

And it did. Carey couldn't think of a single way to get around that one to inquire as to our exact relationship.

I was beginning to wonder about our relationship, myself. Considering the little problem Jane had left me to deal with.

"So, do you plan on living here?" Carey had rallied and was counterattacking with even more directness.

"I don't know." And I didn't add or explain. I liked Carey Osland, but I needed to be by myself with the thing in the window seat.

"Well"—Carey took a deep breath and released it—"I guess I'd better be getting ready for work."

"Thanks for coming by," I said as warmly as I could. "I'm sure I'll be seeing you again when I have things more settled here."

"Like I said, I'm right next door, so if you need me, come on over. My little girl is away at summer camp till this weekend, so I'm all on my own."

"Thanks so much, I may be taking you up on that," I said, trying to beam goodwill and neighborliness enough to soften the fact that I did not want a prolonged conversation and I wanted her gone, things I was afraid I'd made offensively obvious.

My sigh of relief was so loud after I'd shut and locked the door behind her that I hoped she wouldn't hear it.

I sank down into the chair again and covered my face with my hands, preparing to think.

Sweet, fragile, silver-haired Jane Engle, school librarian and churchgoer, had murdered someone and put the victim's skull in her window seat. Then she'd had the window seat carpeted over so no one would think to look there for anything. The carpet was in excellent condition, but not new. Jane had lived in that house with a skull in her living room for some years.

That alone would take some hard getting used to.

I should call the police. My hand actually picked up the receiver before I remembered that the phone was disconnected and that I owed Jane Engle. I owed her big-time.

Jane had left me the house and the money and the skull.

I could not call the police and expose Jane to the world as a murderess. She had counted on that.

Drawn irresistibly, I went to the window seat and opened it again.

"Who the hell are you?" I asked the skull. With considerable squeamishness, I lifted it out with both hands. It wasn't white like bones looked in the movies, but brownish. I didn't know if it was a man's or a woman's skull, but the cause of death seemed apparent; there was a hole in the back of the skull, a hole with jagged edges.

How on earth had elderly Jane managed to deliver such a blow? Who could this be? Perhaps a visitor had fallen and bashed the back of his head on something, and Jane had been afraid she'd be accused of killing the person? That was a familiar and almost comforting plot to a regular mystery reader. Then I thought in a muddled way of *Arsenic and Old Lace*. Perhaps this was a homeless person, or a solitary old man with no family? But Lawrenceton was not large enough for a missing person to go unnoticed, I thought. At least I couldn't recall such a case for years.

Not since Carey Osland's husband had left to pick up diapers and had never returned.

I almost dropped the skull. Oh my Lord! Was this Mike Osland? I put the skull down on Jane's coffee table carefully, as if I might hurt it if I wasn't gentle. And what would I do with it now? I couldn't put it back in the window seat, now that I'd loosened the carpet and made the place conspicuous, and there was no way I could get the carpet to look as smooth as it had been. Maybe now that the house had been burgled, I could hide the skull in one of the places the searcher had already looked?

That raised a whole new slew of questions. Was this skull the thing the searcher had been looking for? If Jane had killed someone, how did anyone else know about it? Why come looking now? Why not just go to the police and say, "Jane Engle has a skull in her house somewhere, I'm certain." No matter how crazy they'd sound, that was what most people would do. Why had this person done otherwise?

This added up to more questions than I answered at the library in a month. Plus, those questions were a lot easier to answer. "Can you recommend a good mystery without any, you know, sex, for my mother?" was a lot easier to answer than "Whose skull is sitting on my coffee table?"

Okay, first things first. Hide the skull. I felt removing it from the house would be safest. (I say "felt" because I was pretty much beyond reasoning.)

I got a brown Kroger bag, from the kitchen and eased the skull into it. I put a can of coffee in another bag, figuring two bags were less conspicuous than one. After rearranging the window seat as best I could, I looked at my watch. It was ten o'clock, and Carey Osland should be at work. I'd seen Torrance Rideout leaving, but, according to what he'd told me the day before, his wife should be at home unless he was running errands.

I peeked through the blinds. The house across from Torrance Rideout's was as still as it had been the day before. The one across from Carey Osland's had two small children playing in the side yard next to Faith Street, a good distance away. All clear. But, even as I watched, a you-do-it moving van pulled up in front of the house across the street.

"Oh, great," I muttered. "Just great." After a moment, though, I decided that the moving van would be far more interesting than my departure if anyone was watching. So, before I could worry about it, I grabbed up my purse and my two paper bags and went out the kitchen door into the carport.

"Aurora?" called a voice incredulously.

With a strong feeling that fate was dealing harshly with me, I turned to the people climbing out of the moving van, to see that my former lover, burglary detective Arthur Smith, and his bride, homicide detective Lynn Liggett, were moving in across the street.

FOUR

FROM BEING BIZARRE and upsetting, my day had moved into surrealistic. I walked on legs that didn't feel like my own toward two police detectives, my purse slung on my shoulder, a can of coffee in the bag in my right hand, a perforated skull in the bag in my left. My hands began sweating. I tried to force a pleasant expression on my face, but had no idea what I had achieved.

Next they're going to say, I thought, they're going to say—*What's in the bag?*

The only plus to meeting up with the very pregnant Mrs. Smith at this moment was that I was so worried about the skull I was not concerned about the awkward personal situation I'd landed in. But I *was* aware—acutely—that I had on no makeup and my hair was restrained with a rubber band.

Arthur's fair skin flushed red, which it did when he was embarrassed, or angry, or—well, no, don't think about that. Arthur was too tough to embarrass easily, but he was embarrassed now.

"Are you visiting here?" Lynn asked hopefully.

"Jane Engle died," I began to explain. "Arthur, you remember Jane?"

He nodded. "The Madeleine Smith expert."

"Jane left me her house," I said, and a childish part of me wanted to add, "and lots and lots of money." But a more mature part of my mind vetoed it, not only because I was carrying a skull in a bag and didn't want to prolong this encounter, but because money was not a legitimate score over Lynn acquiring Arthur. My modern brain told me that a married woman had no edge over an unmarried woman, but my primitive heart knew I would never be "even" with Lynn until I married, myself.

It was a fragmented day in Chez Teagarden.

The Smiths looked dismayed, as well they might. Moving into their little dream home, baby on the way—baby very much on the way—and then the Old Girlfriend appears right across the street.

"I'm not sure whether or not I'll live here," I said before they could ask me. "But I'll be in and out the next week or two getting things straightened out." Could I ever possibly straighten this out?

Lynn sighed. I looked up at her, really seeing her for the first time. Lynn's short brown hair looked lifeless, and, far from glowing with pregnancy, as I'd heard women did, Lynn's skin looked blotchy. But when she turned and looked back at the house, she looked very happy.

"How are you feeling, Lynn?" I asked politely.

"Pretty good. The ultrasound showed the baby is a lot further along than we thought, maybe by seven weeks, so we kind of rushed through buying the house to be sure we got in here and got everything settled before the baby comes."

Just then, thank goodness, a car pulled up behind the van and some men piled out. I recognized them as police pals of Arthur's and Lynn's; they'd come to help unload the van.

Then I realized the man driving the car, the burly man about ten years older than Arthur, was Jack Burns, a detective sergeant, the one of the few people in the world I truly feared.

Here were at least seven policemen, including Jack Burns, and here I was with ... I was scared to even think it with Jack Burns around. His zeal for dealing out punishment to wrongdoers was so sharp, his inner rage burned with such a flame, I felt he could smell concealment and falsehood. My legs began shaking. I was afraid someone would notice. How on earth did his two teenagers manage a private life?

"Good to have seen you," I said abruptly. "I hope your moving day goes as well as they ever do."

They were relieved the encounter was over, too. Arthur gave me a casual wave as a shout from one of his buddies who had opened the back of the van summoned him to work.

"Come see us when we get settled in," Lynn told me insincerely as I said good-bye and turned to leave.

"Take it easy, Lynn," I called over my shoulder, as I crossed the street to my car on rubbery legs.

I put the bags carefully in the front seat and slid in myself. I wanted to sit and shake for a while, but I also wanted to get the hell out of there, so I turned the key in the ignition, turned on the air-conditioning full blast, and occupied a few moments buckling my seat belt, patting my face (which was streaming with sweat) with my handkerchief, anything to give me a little time to calm down before I had to drive. I backed out with great care, the unfamiliar driveway, the moving van parked right across the street, and the people milling around it making the process even more hazardous.

I managed to throw a casual wave in the direction of the moving crew, and some of them waved back. Jack Burns just stared; I wondered again about his wife and children, living with that burning stare that seemed to see all your secrets. Maybe he could switch it off at home? Sometimes even the men under his command seemed leery of him, I'd learned while I was dating Arthur.

I drove around aimlessly for a while, wondering what to do with the skull. I hated to take it to my own home; there was no good hiding place. I couldn't throw it away until I'd decided what to do with it. My safe deposit box at the bank wasn't big enough, and probably Jane's wasn't either: otherwise, surely she would have put the skull there originally. Anyway, the thought of carrying the paper bag into the bank was enough to make me giggle hysterically. I sure couldn't keep it in the trunk of my car. I checked with a glance to make sure my inspection sticker was up-to-date; yes, thank God. But I could be stopped for some traffic violation at any time; I never had been before, but, the way things were going today, it seemed likely.

I had a key to my mother's house, and she was gone.

No sooner had the thought crossed my mind than I turned at the next corner to head there. I wasn't happy about using Mother's house for such a purpose, but it seemed the best thing to do at the time.

The air was dead and hot inside Mother's big home on Plantation Drive. I dashed up the stairs to my old room without thinking, then stood panting in the doorway trying to think of a good hiding place. I kept almost nothing here anymore, and this was really another guest bedroom now, but there might be something up in the closet.

There was: a zippered, pink plastic blanket bag in which Mother always stored the blue blankets for the twin beds in this room. No one would need to get blankets down in this weather. I pulled over the stool from the vanity table, climbed up on it, and unzipped the plastic bag. I took my Kroger bag, with its gruesome contents, and inserted it between the blankets. The bag would no longer zip with the extra bulk.

This was getting grotesque. Well, more grotesque.

I took out one of the blankets and doubled up the other one in half the blanket bag, leaving the other half for the skull. The bag zipped, and it didn't look too lumpy, I decided. I pushed it to the back of the shelf.

Now all I had to dispose of was a blanket. The chest of drawers was only partially full of odds and ends; Mother kept two drawers empty for guests. I stuffed the blanket in one, slammed it shut, then pulled it right back open. She might need the drawer. John was moving all his stuff in when they got back from their honeymoon. I felt like sitting on the floor and bursting into tears. I stood holding the damn blanket indecisively, thinking wildly of burning it or taking it home with me. I'd rather have the blanket than the skull.

The bed, of course. The best place to hide a blanket is on a bed.

I stripped the bedspread off, pitched the pillow on the floor, and fitted the blanket smoothly on the mattress. In a few more minutes, the bed looked exactly like it had before.

I dragged myself out of Mother's house and drove over to my own place. It seemed as though I'd gone two days without sleep, when in fact it was only now getting close to lunchtime. At least I didn't have to go to work this afternoon.

I poured myself a glass of iced tea and for once loaded it with sugar. I sat in my favorite chair and sipped it slowly. It was time to think.

Fact One. Jane Engle had left a skull concealed in her house. She might not have told Bubba Sewell what she'd done, but she'd hinted to him that all was not well—but that I would handle it.

Question: How had the skull gotten in Jane's house? had she murdered its—owner? occupant?

Question: Where was the rest of the skeleton?

Question: How long ago had the head been placed in the window seat?

Fact Two. Someone else knew or suspected that the skull was in Jane's house. I could infer that this someone else was basically law-abiding since the searcher hadn't taken the chance to steal anything or vandalize the house to any degree. The broken window was small potatoes compared with what could have been wreaked on Jane's unoccupied house. So the skull was almost certainly the sole object of the search. Unless Jane had—horrible thought—something else hidden in her house?

Question: Would the searcher try again, or was he perhaps persuaded that the skull was no longer there? The yard had been searched, too, according to Torrance Rideout. I reminded myself to go in the backyard the next time I went to the house and see what had been done there.

Fact Three. I was in a jam. I could keep silent forever, throw the skull in a river, and try to forget I ever saw it; that approach had lots of appeal right now. Or I could take it to the police and tell them what I'd done. I could already feel myself shiver at the thought of Jack Burns's face, to say nothing of the incredulity on Arthur's. I heard myself stammer, "Well, I hid it at my mother's house." What kind of excuse could I offer for my strange actions? Even I could not understand exactly why I'd done what I'd done, except that I'd acted out of some kind of loyalty to Jane, influenced to some extent by all the money she'd left me.

Then and there, I pretty much ruled out going to the police unless something else turned up. I had no idea what my legal position was, but I couldn't imagine what I'd done so far was so very bad legally. Morally was another question.

But I definitely had a problem on my hands.

At this inopportune moment the doorbell rang. It was a day of unwelcome interruptions. I sighed and went to answer it, hoping it was someone I wanted to see. Aubrey?

But the day continued its apparently inexorable downhill slide. Parnell Engle and his wife, Leah, were at my front door, the door no one ever uses because they'd have to park in the back—ten feet from my back door—and then walk all the way around the whole row of town houses to the front to ring the bell. Of course, that was what Parnell and Leah had done.

"Mr. Engle, Mrs. Engle," I said. "Please come in."

Parnell opened fire immediately. "What did we do to Jane, Miss Teagarden? Did she tell you what we did to her that offended her so much she left everything to you?"

I didn't need this.

"Don't you start, Mr. Engle," I said sharply. "Just don't you start. This is *not a good day*. You got a car, you got some money, you got Madeleine the cat. Just be glad of it and leave me alone."

"We were Jane's own blood kin—"

"Don't start with me," I snapped. I was simply beyond trying to be polite. "I don't know why she left everything to me, but it doesn't make me feel very lucky right now, believe me."

"We realize," he said with less whine and more dignity, "that Jane did express her true wishes in her will. We know that she was in her good senses up until the end and that she made her choice knowing what she was doing. We're not going to contest the will. We just don't understand it."

"Well, Mr. Engle, neither do I." Parnell would have had that skull at the police station in less time than it takes to talk about it. But it was good news that they weren't small-minded enough to contest the will and thereby cause me endless trouble and heartache. I knew Lawrenceton. Pretty soon people would start saying, Well, why *did* Jane Engle leave everything to a young woman she didn't even know very well? And speculation would run rampant; I couldn't even imagine the things people would make up to explain Jane's inexplicable legacy. People were going to talk anyway, but any dispute about the will would put a nasty twist on that speculation.

Looking at Parnell Engle and his silent wife, with their dowdy clothes and grievances, I suddenly wondered if I'd gotten the money to pay me for the inconvenience of the skull. What Jane had told Bubba Sewell might have been just a smoke screen. She may have read my character thoroughly, almost supernaturally thoroughly, and known I would keep her secret.

"Good-bye," I said to them gently, and closed my front door slowly, so they couldn't say I'd slammed it on them. I locked it carefully, and marched to my telephone. I looked up Bubba Sewell's number and dialed. He was in and available, to my surprise.

"How's things going, Miss Teagarden?" he drawled.

"Kind of bumpy, Mr. Sewell."

"Sorry to hear that. How can I be of assistance?"

"Did Jane leave me a letter?"

"What?"

"A letter, Mr. Sewell. Did she leave me a letter, something I'm supposed to get after I've had the house a month, or something?"

"No, Miss Teagarden."

"Not a cassette? No tape of any kind?"

"No, ma'am."

"Did you see anything like that in the safe deposit box?"

"No, no, can't say as I did. Actually, I just rented that box after Jane became so ill, to put her good jewelry in."

"And she didn't tell you what was in the house?" I asked carefully.

"Miss Teagarden, I have no idea what's in Miss Engle's house," he said definitely. Very definitely.

I stopped, baffled. Bubba Sewell didn't want to know. If I told him, he might have to do something about it, and I hadn't yet decided what should be done.

"Thanks," I said hopelessly. "Oh, by the way..." And I told him about Parnell and Leah's visit.

"He said for sure they weren't going to contest?"

"He said they knew that Jane was in her right mind when she made her will, that they just wanted to know why she left everything the way she did."

"But he didn't talk about going to court or getting his own lawyer?"

"No."

"Let's just hope he meant it when he said he knew Jane was in her right mind when she made her will."

On that happy note we told each other good-bye.

I returned to my chair and tried to pick up the thread of my reasoning. Soon I realized I'd gone as far as I could go.

It seemed to me that if I could find out who the skull had belonged to, I'd have a clearer course to follow. I could start by finding out how long the skull had been in the window seat. If Jane had kept the bill from the carpet layers, that would give me a definite date, because the skull had for sure been in the window seat when the carpet was installed over it. And it hadn't been disturbed since.

That meant I had to go back to Jane's house.

I sighed deeply.

I might as well have some lunch, collect some boxes, and go to work at the house this afternoon as I'd planned originally.

This time yesterday I'd been a woman with a happy future; now I was a woman with a secret, and it was such a strange, macabre secret that I felt I had GUILTY KNOWLEDGE written on my forehead.

THE UNLOADING across the street was still going on. I saw a large carton labeled with a picture of a baby crib being carried in, and almost wept. But I had other things to do today than beat myself over the head with losing Arthur. That grief had a stale, preoccupied feel to it.

The disorder in Jane's bedroom had to be cleared away before I could think about finding her papers. I carried in my boxes, found the coffeepot, and started the coffee (which I'd brought back, since I had carried it away in the morning) to perking. The house was so cool and so quiet that it almost made me drowsy. I turned on Jane's bedside radio; yuck, it was on the easy listening station. I found the public radio station after a second's search, and began to pack clothes to Beethoven. I searched each garment as I packed, just on the off chance I would find something that would explain the hidden skull. I just could not believe Jane would leave me this problem with no explanation.

Maybe she'd thought I'd never find it?

No, Jane had thought I'd find it sooner or later. Maybe not this soon. But sometime. Perhaps, if it hadn't been for the break-in, and the holes in the backyard (and here I reminded myself again to check them), I wouldn't have worried about a thing, no matter how mysterious some of Bubba Sewell's statements had been.

Suddenly I thought of the old saw "You don't look a gift horse in the mouth." I recalled the skull's grin all too clearly, and I began laughing.

I had to laugh at something.

It didn't take quite as long as I expected to pack Jane's clothes. If something had struck my fancy, it wouldn't have bothered me to keep it; Jane had been a down-to-earth woman, and in some ways I supposed I was, too. But I saw nothing I wanted to keep except a cardigan or two, so anonymous that I wouldn't be constantly thinking, I am wearing Jane's clothes. So all the dresses and blouses, coats and shoes and skirts that had been in the closet were neatly boxed and ready to go to the Goodwill, with the vexing exception of a robe that slipped from its hanger to the floor. Every box was full to the brim, so I just left it where it fell. I loaded the boxes into my car trunk, then decided to take a break by strolling into the backyard and seeing what damage had been done there.

Jane's backyard was laid out neatly. There were two concrete benches, too hot to sit on in the June sun, placed on either side of a concrete birdbath surrounded by monkey grass. The monkey grass was getting out of hand, I noticed. Someone else had thought so, too; a big chunk of it had been uprooted. I'd dealt with monkey grass before and admired the unknown gardener's persistence. Then it came to me that this was one of the "dug up" spots that Torrance Rideout had filled in for me. Looking around me more carefully, I saw a few more; all were around bushes, or under the two benches. None were out in the middle of the grass, which was a relief. I had to just shake my head over this; someone had seriously thought Jane had dug a hole out in her yard and stuck the skull in it? A pretty futile search after all this time Jane had had the skull.

That was a sobering thought. Desperate people are not gentle.

As I mooched around the neat little yard, counting the holes around the bushes that had screened the unattractive school fence from Jane's view, I became aware of movement in the Rideouts' backyard. Minimal movement. A woman was sunbathing on the huge sun deck in a lounge chair, a woman with a long, slim body already deeply browned and semiclad in a fire engine red bikini. Her chin-length, dyed, pale blond hair was held back by a matching band, and even her fingernails seemed to be the same shade of red. She was awfully turned out for sunbathing on her own deck, presuming this was Marcia Rideout.

"How are you, new neighbor?" she called languidly, a slim brown arm raising a glass of iced tea to her lips. This was the movement I'd glimpsed.

"Fine," I lied automatically. "And you?"

"Getting along, getting by." She beckoned with a lazy wave. "Come talk for a minute."

When I was settled in a chair beside her, she extended a thin hand and said, "Marcia Rideout."

"Aurora Teagarden," I murmured as I shook her hand, and the amusement flitted across her face and vanished. She pulled off her opaque sunglasses and gave me a direct look. Her eyes were dark blue, and she was drunk, or at least on her way there. Maybe she saw something in my face, because she popped the sunglasses right back on. I tried not to peer at her drink; I suspected it was not tea at all, but bourbon.

"Would you like something to drink?" Marcia Rideout offered.

"No thanks," I said hastily.

"So you inherited the house. Think you'll like living there?"

"I don't know if I will live there," I told her, watching her fingers run up and down the dripping glass. She took another sip.

"I drink sometimes," she told me frankly.

I really couldn't think of anything to say.

"But only when Torrance isn't coming home. He has to spend the night on the road sometimes, maybe once every two weeks or so. And those days he's not coming home to spend the night, I drink. Very slowly."

"I expect you get lonely," I offered uncertainly.

She nodded. "I expect I do. Now, Carey Osland on the other side of you, and Macon Turner on the other side of me, *they* don't get lonely. Macon sneaks over there through the backyards, some nights."

"He must be an old-fashioned guy." There was nothing to prevent Macon and Carey from enjoying each other's company. Macon was divorced and Carey was, too, presumably, unless Mike Osland was dead . . . and that reminded me of the skull, which I had enjoyed forgetting for a moment.

My comment struck Marcia Rideout as funny. As I watched her laugh, I saw she had more wrinkles than I'd figured, and I upped her age by maybe seven years. But from her body you sure couldn't tell it.

"I didn't used to have such a problem with being lonely," Marcia said slowly, her amusement over. "We used to have people renting this apartment." She waved in the direction of the garage with its little room on top. "One time it was a high school teacher, I liked her. Then she got another job and moved. Then it was Ben Greer, that jerk that works at the grocery chopping meat—you know him?"

"Yeah. He is a jerk."

"So I was glad when he moved. Then we had a housepainter, Mark Kaplan..." She seemed to be drifting off, and I thought her eyes closed behind the dark glasses.

"What happened to him?" I asked politely.

"Oh. He was the only one who ever left in the night without paying the rent."

"Gosh. Just skipped out? Bag and baggage?" Maybe another candidate for the skull?

"Yep. Well, he took some of his stuff. He never came back for the rest. You sure you don't want a drink? I have some real tea, you know."

Unexpectedly, Marcia smiled, and I smiled back.

"No, thanks. You were saying about your tenant?"

"He ran out. And we haven't had anyone since. Torrance just doesn't want to fool with it. The past couple of years, he's gotten like that. I tell him he must be middle-aged. He and Jane and their big fight over that tree!"

I followed Marcia's pointing red-tipped finger. There was a tree just about midway between the houses. It had a curiously lopsided appearance, viewed from the Rideouts' deck.

"It's just about straddling the property line," Marcia said. She had a slow, deep voice, very attractive. "You won't believe, if you've got any sense, that people could fight about a tree."

"People can fight about anything. I've been managing some apartments, and the tizzy people get into if someone uses their parking space!"

"Really, I can believe it. Well, as you can see, the tree is a little closer to Jane's house...your house." Marcia took another sip from her drink. "But Torrance didn't like those leaves, he got sick of raking them. So he talked to Jane about taking the tree down. It wasn't shading either house, really. Well, Jane had a fit. She really got hot. So Torrance just cut the branches that were over our property line. Ooo, Jane stomped over here the next day, and she said, 'Now, Torrance Rideout, that was petty. I have a bone to pick with you.' I wonder what the origin of that saying is? You happen to know?"

I shook my head, fascinated with the little story and Marcia's digression.

"There wasn't any putting the branches back, they were cut to hell," said Marcia flatly, her southern accent roughening. "And somehow Torrance got Jane calmed down. But things never were the same after that, between Torrance and Jane. But Jane and I still spoke, and we were on the board of the orphans' home together. I liked her."

I had a hard time picturing Jane that angry. Jane had been a pleasant person, even sweet occasionally, always polite: but she was also extremely conscious of personal property, rather like my mother.

Jane didn't have or want much in the way of things, but what she had was hers absolutely, not to be touched by other hands without proper permission being asked and granted. I saw from Marcia's little story how far that sense of property went. I was learning a lot about Jane now that it was too late. I hadn't known she'd been on the board of the orphans' home, actually and less bluntly named Mortimer House.

"Well," Marcia continued slowly, "at least the past couple of years they'd been getting along fine, Jane and Torrance...she forgave him, I guess. I'm sleepy now."

"I'm sorry you had the trouble with Jane," I said, feeling that somehow I should apologize for my benefactress. "She was always such an intelligent, interesting person." I stood to leave; Marcia's eyes were closed behind her sunglasses, I thought.

"Shoot, the fight she had with Torrance was nothin', you should have heard her and Carey go to it."

"When was that?" I asked, trying to sound indifferent.

But Marcia Rideout was asleep, her hand still wrapped around her drink.

I trudged back to my task, sweating in the sun, worried about Marcia burning since she'd fallen asleep on the lounge. But she'd been slathered with oil. I made a mental note to look out the back from time to time to see if she was still there.

It was hard for me to picture Jane being furious with anyone and marching over to tell him about it. Of course, I'd never owned property. Maybe I would be the same way now. Neighbors could get very upset over things uninvolved people would laugh about. I remembered my mother, a cool and elegant Lauren Bacall type, telling me she was going to buy a rifle and shoot her neighbor's dog if it woke her up with its barking again. She had gone to the police instead and gotten a court order against the dog's owner after the police chief, an old friend, had come to her house and sat in the dark listening to the dog yapping one night. The dog's owner hadn't spoken to Mother since, and in fact had been transferred to another city, without the slightest sign of their mutual disgust slackening.

I wondered what Jane had fought with Carey about. It was hard to see how this could relate to my immediate problem, the skull; it sure wasn't the skull of Carey Osland or Torrance Rideout. I couldn't imagine Jane killing the Rideouts' tenant, Mark whatever-his-name-was, but at least I had the name of another person who might be The Skull.

Back in my house once again—I was practicing saying "my house"—I began to search for Jane's papers. Everyone had some cache of cancelled checks, old receipts, car papers, and tax stuff. I found Jane's in the guest bedroom, sorted into floral-patterned cardboard boxes by year. Jane kept everything, and she kept all those papers for seven years, I discovered. I sighed, swore, and opened the first box.

FIVE

I PLUGGED IN JANE'S television and listened to the news with one ear while I went through Jane's papers. Apparently all the papers to do with the car had already been handed over to Parnell Engle, for there were no old inspection receipts or anything like that. It would have helped if Jane had kept all these papers in some kind of category, I told myself grumpily, trying not to think of my own jumble of papers in shoe boxes in my closet.

I'd started with the earliest box, dated seven years ago. Jane had kept receipts that surely could be thrown away now; dresses she'd bought, visits by the bug-spray man, the purchase of a telephone. I began sorting as I looked, the pile of definite discards getting higher and higher.

There's a certain pleasure in throwing things away. I was concentrating contentedly, so it took me awhile to realize I was hearing some kind of sound from outside. Someone seemed to be doing something to the screen door in the kitchen. I sat hunched on the living room floor, listening with every molecule. I reached over and switched off the television. Gradually I relaxed. Whatever was being done, it wasn't being done surreptitiously. Whatever the sound was, it escalated.

I stiffened my spine and went to investigate. I opened the wooden door cautiously, just as the noise repeated. Hanging spread-eagled on the screen door was a very large, very fat orange cat. This seemed to explain the funny snags I'd noticed on the screen when I went in the backyard earlier.

"Madeleine?" I said in amazement.

The cat gave a dismal yowl and dropped from the screen to the top step. Unthinkingly, I opened the door, and Madeleine was in in a flash.

"You wouldn't think a cat so fat could move so fast," I said.

Madeleine was busy stalking through her house, sniffing and rubbing her side against the door frames.

To say I was in a snit would be putting it mildly. This cat was now Parnell and Leah's. Jane knew I was not partial to pets, not at all. My mother had never let me have one, and gradually her convictions about pet hygiene and inconvenience had influenced me. Now I would have to call Parnell, talk with him again, either take the cat to him or get him to come get the cat...she would probably scratch me if I tried to put her in my car...another complication in my life. I sank into one of the kitchen chairs and rested my head on my hands dismally.

Madeleine completed her house tour and came and sat in front of me, her front paws neatly covered by her plumy tail. She looked up at me expectantly. Her eyes were round and gold and had a kind of stare that reminded me of Arthur Smith's. That stare said, "I am the toughest and the baddest, don't mess with me." I found myself giving a halfhearted chuckle at Madeleine's machisma. Suddenly she crouched, and in one fluid movement shifted her bulk from the floor to the table—where Jane *ate*! I thought, horrified.

She could stare at me more effectively there. Growing impatient at my stupidity, Madeleine butted her golden head against my hand. I patted her uncertainly. She still seemed to be waiting for something. I tried to picture Jane with the cat, and I seemed to recall she'd scratched the animal behind the ears. I tried that. A deep rumble percolated somewhere in Madeleine's insides. The cat's eyes half-closed with pleasure. Encouraged by this response, I kept scratching her gently behind the ears, then switched to the area under her chin. This, too, was popular.

I grew tired of this after a while and stopped. Madeleine stretched, yawned, and jumped heavily down from the table. She walked over to one of the cabinets, and sat in front of it, casting a significant look over her shoulder at me. Fool that I am, it took me a few minutes to get the message. Made-

leine gave a soprano yowl. I opened the bottom
cabinet, and saw only the pots and pans I'd re-
loaded the day before. Madeleine kept her stare
steady. She seemed to feel I was a slow learner. I
looked in the cabinets above the counter and found
some canned cat food. I looked down at Madeleine and said brightly, "This what you wanted?"
She yowled again and began to pace back and
forth, her eyes never leaving the black and green
can. I hunted down the electric can opener, plugged
it in, and used it. With a flourish, I set the can down
on the floor. After a moment's dubious pause—she
clearly wasn't used to eating from a can—Madeleine dived in. After a little more searching, I filled
a plastic bowl with water and put it down by the
can. This, too, met with the cat's approval.

I went to the phone to call Parnell, my feet dragging reluctantly. But of course I hadn't had the
phone hooked up. I reminded myself again I'd have
to do something about that, and looked at the cat,
now grooming herself with great concentration.
"What am I going to do with you?" I muttered. I
decided I'd leave her here for the night and call
Parnell from my place. He could come get her in
the morning. Somehow I hated to put her outside;
she was an inside cat for the most part, I seemed to
remember Jane telling me...though frankly I'd
often tuned out when Jane chatted about the cat.
Pet owners could be such bores. Madeleine would

need a litter box; Jane had had one tucked away beside the refrigerator. It wasn't there now. Maybe it had been taken to the vet's where Madeleine had been boarded during Jane's illness. It was probably sitting uselessly at the Engles' house now.

I poked around in the trash left in Jane's room from my cleaning out the closet. Sure enough, there was a box of the appropriate size and shape. I put it in the corner by the refrigerator in the kitchen, and as Madeleine watched with keen attention I opened cabinets until I found a half-full bag of cat litter.

I felt rather proud of myself at handling the little problem the cat presented so quickly; though, when I considered, it seemed Madeleine had done all the handling. She had gotten back to her old home, gained entrance, been fed and watered, and had a toilet provided her, and now she jumped up on Jane's armchair in the living room, curled into a striped orange ball, and went to sleep. I watched her for a moment enviously, then I sighed and began sorting papers again.

In the fourth box I found what I wanted. The carpet had been installed three years ago. So the skull had become a skull sometime before that. Suddenly I realized what should have been obvious. Of course Jane had not killed someone and put his head in the window seat fresh, so to speak. The skull had already been a skull, not a head, before

Jane had sealed it up. I was willing to concede that Jane obviously had a side unknown to me, or to anyone, though whoever had searched the house must at least suspect it. But I could not believe that Jane would live in a house with a decomposing head in the window seat. Jane had not been a monster.

What had Jane been? I pulled up my knees and wrapped my arms around them. Behind me, Madeleine, who had observed Jane longer than anyone, yawned and rearranged herself.

Jane had been a woman in her late seventies with silver hair almost always done up in a regal chignon. She had never worn slacks, always dresses. She had had a lively mind—an intelligent mind—and good manners. She had been interested in true crime, at a safe distance; her favorite cases were all Victorian or earlier. She had had a mother who was wealthy and who had held a prominent place in Lawrenceton society, and Jane had behaved as though she herself had neither. She had inherited from somewhere, though, a strong sense of property. But as far as the liberation of women went— well, Jane and I had had some discussions on that. Jane was a traditionalist, and though as a working woman she had believed in equal pay for equal work, some of the other tenets of the women's movement were lost on her. "Women don't have to confront men, honey," she'd told me one time.

"Women can always think their way around them."
Jane had not been a forgiving person, either; if she
got really angry and did not receive an adequate
apology, she held a grudge a good long while. She
was not even aware of grudge holding, I'd observed; if she had been, she would have fought it,
like she'd fought other traits in herself she didn't
think were Christian. What else had Jane been?
Conventionally moral, dependable, and she'd had
an unexpectedly sly sense of humor.

In fact, wherever Jane was now, I was willing to
bet she was looking at me and laughing. Me, with
Jane's money and Jane's house and Jane's cat and
Jane's skull.

AFTER SORTING MORE PAPERS (I might as well finish what I've begun, I thought), I got up to stretch.
It was raining outside, I discovered to my surprise.
As I sat on the window seat and looked out the
blinds, the rain got heavier and heavier and the
thunder started to boom. The lights came on across
the street in the little white house with yellow shutters, and through the front window I could see
Lynn unpacking boxes, moving slowly and awk-
wardly. I wondered how having a baby felt, wondered if I would ever know. Finally, for no reason
that I could discern, my feeling for Arthur ended,
and the pain drained away. Tired of poring over
receipts left from a life that was over, I thought

about my own life. Living by myself was sometimes fun, but I didn't want to do it forever, as Jane
had. I thought of Robin Crusoe, the mystery writer,
who had left town when my romance with Arthur
had heated up. I thought of Aubrey Scott. I was
tired of being alone with my bizarre problem. I was
tired of being alone, period.

I told myself to switch mental tracks in a hurry.
There was something undeniably pleasant about
being in my own house watching the rain come
down outside, knowing I didn't have to go anywhere if I didn't want to. I was surrounded by
books in a pretty room, I could occupy myself
however I chose. Come on, I asked myself bravely,
what do you choose to do? I almost chose to start
crying, but instead I jumped up, found Jane's Soft
Scrub, and cleaned the bathroom. A place isn't really yours unfil you clean it. Jane's place became
mine, however temporarily, that afternoon. I
cleaned and sorted and threw away and inventoried. I opened a can of soup and heated it in my
saucepan on my stove. I ate it with my spoon.
Madeleine came into the kitchen when she heard me
bustling around and jumped up to watch me eat.
This time I was not horrified. I looked over the
book I'd pulled from Jane's shelves and addressed
a few remarks to Madeleine while I ate.

It was still raining after I'd washed the pot and
the spoon and the bowl, so I sat in Jane's chair in

the living room, watching the rain and wondering what to do next. After a moment, the cat heaved herself up onto my lap. I wasn't quite sure how I felt about this liberty on the cat's part, but I decided I'd give it a try. I stroked the smooth fur tentatively and heard the deep percolation start up. What I needed, I decided, was to talk to someone who knew Lawrenceton in depth, someone who knew about Carey Osland's husband and the Rideouts' tenant. I'd been assuming the skull came from someone who lived close by, and suddenly I realized I'd better challenge that assumption.

Why had I thought that? There had to be a reason. Okay—Jane couldn't transport a body any distance. I just didn't think she'd been strong enough. But I remembered the hole in the skull and shuddered, feeling distinctly queasy for a moment. She'd been strong enough to do that. Had Jane herself cut off the head? I couldn't even picture it. Granted, Jane's bookshelves, like mine, were full of accounts about people who had done horrible things and gone unsuspected for long periods of time, but I just couldn't admit Jane might be like that. Something wasn't adding up.

It just might be my own dearly held assumptions and preconceptions. Jane, after all, was a Little Old Lady.

I was worn out physically and mentally. It was time to go back to my place. I unseated the cat, to her disgust, and filled her water dish, while making a mental note to call Parnell. I stuffed my car full of things to throw or give away, locked up, and left.

For Christmas, my mother had given me an answering machine, and its light was blinking when I let myself into my kitchen. I leaned against the counter while I punched the button to hear my messages.

"Roe, this is Aubrey. Sorry I didn't catch you in. I'll talk to you later. See you at church tomorrow?"

Ah oh. Tomorrow was Sunday. Maybe I should go to the Episcopal church. But since I didn't always go there, wouldn't it look a little pointed to show up right after I'd had a date with the pastor? On the other hand, here he was inviting me personally, and I'd hurt his feelings if I didn't show...oh hell.

"Hi, honey! We're having such a good time John and I decided to stay for a few more days! Stop by the office and make sure everyone's busy, okay? I'll be calling Eileen, but I think it would impress everyone if you went yourself. Talk to you later! Wait till you see my tan!"

Everyone at Mother's office knew that I was strictly an underling, and that I didn't know jack about the real estate business, though it wasn't uninteresting. I just didn't want to work full-time for

Mother. Well, I was glad she was having a great time on her second (literally) honeymoon, and I was glad she'd finally taken a vacation of any sort. Eileen Norris, her second-in-command, was probably ready for Mother to come back. Mother's force of character and charm really smoothed things over.

"Roe, this is Robin." I caught my breath and practically hugged the answering machine so I wouldn't miss a word. "I'm leaving tonight for maybe three weeks in Europe, traveling cheap and with no reservations, so I don't know where I'll be when. I won't be working at the university next year. James Artis is over his heart attack. So I'm not sure what I'll be doing. I'll get in touch when I come back. Are you doing okay? How's Arthur?"

"He's married," I said to the machine. "He married someone else."

I rummaged in my junk drawer frantically. "Where's the address book? Where's the damn book?" I muttered. My scrabbling fingers finally found it, I searched through it, got the right page, punched the numbers frantically.

Ring. Ring. "Hello?" a man said.

"Robin?"

"No, this is Phil. I'm subleasing Robin's apartment. He's left for Europe."

"Oh, no," I wailed.

"Can I take a message?" the voice asked, tactfully ignoring my distress.

"So he's going to be coming back to that apartment when he returns? For sure?"

"Yep, his stuff is all here."

"Are you reliable? Can you give him a message in three weeks, or whenever he comes back?"

"I'll try," the voice said with some amusement.

"This is important," I warned him. "To me, anyway."

"Okay, shoot. I've got a pencil and paper right here."

"Tell Robin," I said, thinking as I spoke, "that Roe, R-O-E, is fine."

"Roe is fine," repeated the voice obediently.

"Also say," I continued, "that Arthur married Lynn."

"Okay, got it . . . anything else?"

"No, no thank you. That's all. Just as long as he knows that."

"Well, this is a fresh legal pad, and I've labeled it 'Robin's Messages,' and I'll keep it here by the phone until he comes back," said Phil's voice reassuringly.

"I'm sorry to sound so—well, like I think you'll throw it in the wastebasket—but this is the only way I have to get in touch with him."

"Oh, I understand," said Phil politely. "And really, he will get this."

"Thanks," I said weakly. "I appreciate it."

"Good-bye," said Phil.

"PARNELL? This is Aurora Teagarden."

"Oh. Well, what can I do for you?"

"Madeleine showed up at Jane's house today."

"That dang cat! We've been looking for her high and low. We missed her two days ago, and we were feeling real bad, since Jane was so crazy about that durn animal."

"Well, she came home."

"We sure got a problem. She won't stay here, Aurora. We've caught up with her twice when she started off, but we can't keep chasing after her. As a matter of fact, we're leaving town tomorrow for two weeks, going to our summer place at Beaufort, South Carolina, and we were going to check her back in the vet's, just to make sure everything went okay. Though animals mostly take care of themselves."

Take care of themselves? The Engles expected pampered Madeleine to catch her own fish and mice for two weeks?

"Is that right?" I said, letting incredulity drip from my voice. "No, I expect she can stay at the house for that two weeks. I can feed her when I go over there and empty her litter box."

"Well," said Parnell doubtfully, "her time's almost up."

The cat was dying? Oh my Lord. "That's what the vet said?" I asked in amazement.

"Yes, ma'am," Parnell said, sounding equally amazed.

"She sure looks fat for a cat that sick," I said doubtfully.

I could not understand why Parnell Engle suddenly began laughing. His laugh was a little hoarse and rusty, but it was from the belly.

"Yes, ma'am," he agreed with a little wheeze of joy, "Madeleine is fat for a cat that's so sick."

"I'll keep her then," I said uncertainly.

"Oh, yes, Miss Teagarden, thanks. We'll see you when we come back."

He was still barely controlling his chuckles when he hung up. I put down the receiver and shook my head. There was just no accounting for some people.

SIX

As I RETRIEVED my Sunday paper from my seldom-used front doorstep, I could tell it was already at least 83 degrees. The paper predicted 98 for the day, and I thought its forecast was modest. My central air was already humming. I showered and reluctantly put my hair up in hot curlers, trying to bring order into chaos. I poured my coffee and ate breakfast (a microwaved sweet roll) while I burrowed through the news. I love Sunday mornings, if I get up early enough to really enjoy my paper. Though I have my limits: I will only read the society section if I think my mother will be in it, and I will not read anything about next season's fashions. Amina Day's mom owned a women's clothing shop she had named Great Day, and I pretty much let her tell me what to buy. Under Mrs. Day's influence I'd begun to weed out my librarian clothes, my solid-color interchangeable blouses and skirts. My wardrobe was a bit more diverse now.

The paper exhausted, I padded up the stairs and washed my glasses in the sink. While they dried, I squinted myopically into my closet. What was suitable for the girlfriend of the minister? Long sleeves sounded mandatory, but it was just too hot. I scooted hangers along the bar, humming tunelessly to myself. Shouldn't the girlfriend of the minister be perky but modest? Though perhaps, at nearly thirty, I was a bit old to be perky.

For a dizzying moment I imagined all the clothes I could buy with my inheritance. I had to give myself a little shake to come back to reality and review my wardrobe of the here and now. Here we go! A sleeveless navy blue shirtwaist with big white flowers printed on it. It had a full skirt and a white collar and belt. Just the thing, with my white purse and sandals.

All dressed, with my makeup on, I popped on my glasses and surveyed the result. My hair had calmed down enough to be conventional, and the sandals made my legs look longer. They were hell to walk in, though, and my tolerance time for the high heels would expire right after church.

I walked as quickly as I safely could from my back door across the patio, out the gate in the fence around it, to the car under the long roof that sheltered all tenants' cars. I unlocked the driver's door and flung it open to let the heat blast escape. After a minute I climbed in, and the air conditioner came on one second after the motor. I had worked too hard on my appearance to arrive at the Episcopal church with sweat running down my face.

I accepted a bulletin from an usher and seated myself a carefully calculated distance from the pulpit. The middle-aged couple on the other end of the pew eyed me with open interest and gave me welcoming smiles. I smiled back before becoming immersed in figuring out the hymn and prayer book directions. A loud chord signaled the entrance of the priest, acolyte, lay reader, and choir, and I rose with the rest of the congregation.

Aubrey was just beautiful in his vestments. I drifted into an intoxicating daydream of myself as a minister's wife. It felt very odd to have kissed the man conducting the service. Then I got too involved in managing the prayer book to think about Aubrey for a while. One thing about the Episcopalians, they can't go to sleep during the service unless they're catnappers. You have to get up and down too often, and shake people's hands, and respond, and go up to the altar rail for communion. It's a busy service, not a spectator sport like in some churches. And I believed I had been to every church in Lawrenceton, except maybe one or two of the black ones.

I tried to listen with great attention to Aubrey's sermon, since I would surely have to make an intelligent comment later. To my pleasure, it was an excellent sermon, with some solid points about people's business relationships and how they should conform to religious teachings, too, just as much as personal relationships. And he didn't use a single sports simile! I kept my eyes carefully downcast when I went up to take communion, and tried to think about God rather than Aubrey when he pressed the wafer into my hand.

As we were folding up our kneelers, I saw one of the couples who had spoken to Aubrey while he and I were in line at the movies. They gave me a smile and wave, and huddled to talk to the man and woman with whom I'd been sharing a pew. After that, I was beamed on even more radiantly, and the movie couple introduced me to the pew couple, who asked me about twenty questions as rapidly as they could so they'd have the whole scoop on the pastor's honey.

I felt like I was flying under false colors—we'd only had one date. I began to wish I hadn't come, but Aubrey'd asked me, and I had enjoyed the service. It seemed now I had to pay for it, since there was no quick exit. The crowd had bottle-necked around the church door, shaking hands and exchanging small talk with Aubrey.

"What a good sermon," I told him warmly, when it was finally my turn. My hand was taken in both of his for a moment, pressed and released. A smooth gesture, in one quick turn showing me I was special, yet not presuming too much.

"Thanks, and thanks for coming," he said. "If you're going to be home this afternoon, I'll give you a call."

"If I'm not there, just leave a message on my machine and I'll call you back. I may have to go over to the house."

He understood I meant Jane's house, and nodded, turning to the old lady behind me in line with a happy "Hi, Laura! How's the arthritis?"

Leaving the church parking lot, I felt a distinct letdown. I guess I had hoped Aubrey would ask me to Sunday lunch, a big social event in Lawrenceton. My mother always had me over to lunch when she was home, and I wondered, not for the first time, if she'd still want me to come over when she and John Queensland got back from their honeymoon. John belonged to the country club. He might want to take Mother out there.

I was so dismal by the time I unlocked my back door that I was actually glad to see the message light blinking on the answering machine.

"Hi, Roe. It's Sally Allison. Long time no see, kiddo! Listen, what's this I heard about you inheriting a fortune? Come have lunch with me today if this catches you in time, or give me a call when you can, we'll set up a time."

I opened the book to the *A*'s, looked up Sally's number, and punched the right buttons.

"Hello!"

"Sally, I just got your message."

"Great! You free for lunch since your mom is still out of town?"

Sally knew *everything*.

"Well, yes, I am. What do you have in mind?"

"Oh, come on over here. Out of sheer boredom, I have cooked a roast and baked potatoes and made a salad. I want to share it with someone."

Sally was a woman on her own, like me. But she was divorced, and a good fifteen years older.

"Be there in twenty minutes, I need to change. My feet are killing me."

"Well, wear whatever you see when you open your closet. I have on my oldest shorts."

"Okay, bye."

I shucked off the blue and white dress and those painful sandals. I pulled on olive drab shorts and a jungle print blouse and my huaraches and pounded back down the stairs. I made it to Sally's in the twenty minutes.

SALLY is a newspaper reporter, the veteran of an early runaway marriage that left her with a son to raise and a reputation to make. She was a good reporter, and she'd hoped (a little over a year ago) that reporting the multiple murders in Lawrenceton would net her a better job offer from Atlanta; but it hadn't happened. Sally was insatiably curious and knew everyone in town, and everyone knew that, to get the straight story on anything, Sally was the person to see. We'd had our ups and downs as friends, the ups having been when we were both members of Real Murders, the downs having mostly been at the same time Sally was trying to make a national, or at least regional, name for herself. She'd sacrificed a lot in that bid for a life in the bigger picture, and, when the bid hadn't been taken up, she'd had a hard time. But now Sally was mending her fences locally, and was as plugged in to the Lawrenceton power system as she ever had been. If her stories being picked up by the wire services hadn't gotten her out of the town, it had certainly added to her power in it.

I had always seen Sally very well dressed, in expensive suits and shoes that lasted her a very long time. When I reached her house, I saw Sally was a woman who put her money on her back, as the saying goes. She had a little place not quite as nice as Jane's, in a neighborhood where the lawns weren't kept as well. Her car, which hadn't been washed in weeks, sat in dusty splendor uncovered by carport or garage. Getting in it would be like climbing in an oven. But the house itself was cool enough, no central air but several window air conditioners sending out an icy stream that almost froze the sweat on my forehead.

Sally's hair was as perfect as ever. It looked like it could be taken off and put on without one bronze curl being dislodged. But instead of her usual classic suits, Sally was wearing a pair of cutoffs and an old work shirt.

"Girl, it's hot!" she exclaimed as she let me in. "I'm glad I don't have to work today."

"It's a good day to stay inside," I agreed, looking around me curiously. I'd never been in Sally's house before. It was obvious she didn't give a damn about decor. The couch and armchairs were covered by throws that looked very unfortunate, and the cheap coffee table had rings on top. My resident manager's eye told me that the whole place needed painting. But the bookcase was wonderfully stuffed with Sally's favorite Organized Crime books, and the smell coming from the kitchen was delicious. My mouth watered.

Of course I was going to have to pay for my dinner with information, but it just might be worth it.

"Boy, that smells good! When's it going to be on the table?"

"I'm making the gravy now. Come on back and talk to me while I stir. Want a beer? I've got some ice cold."

"Sure, I'll take one. It's the 'ice cold' that does it."

"Here, drink some ice water first for your thirst. Then sip the beer for your pleasure."

I gulped down the glass of ice water and twisted the cap off the beer. Sally had put out one of those round plastic grippers without my even having to ask. I closed my eyes to appreciate the beer going down my throat. I don't drink beer any other time of the year, but summer in the South is what beer was made for. Very cold beer. "Ooo," I murmured blissfully.

"I know. If I didn't watch out, I could drink a whole six-pack while I cooked."

"Can I set the table or anything?"

"No, I already got everything done, I think. Soon as this gravy is ready—whoa, let me look at the biscuits—yep, they're nice and brown—we'll be ready to eat. Did I get the butter out?"

I scanned the table, which at least was a few feet from the stove. Sally must have been burning up over there.

"It's here," I reassured her.

"Okay, here we go. Roast, biscuits, baked potatoes, a salad, and for desert"—Sally took off a cake cover with a flourish—"red velvet cake!"

"Sally, you're inspired. I haven't had red velvet cake in ten years."

"My mama's recipe."

"Those are always the best. You're so smart." A good southern compliment that could mean almost anything, but this time I meant it quite sincerely. I am not a person who often cooks whole meals for herself. I know single people are supposed to cook full meals, lay the table, and act like they had company, really—but how many single people actually do it? Like Sally, when I cook a big meal, I want someone else to appreciate it and enjoy it.

"So, what's this about you and the man of the cloth?"

Closing in for the kill already. "Sally, you need to wait till I've eaten something," I said. Was the roast worth it?

"What?"

"Oh Sally, it's really nothing. I've have one date with Aubrey Scott, we went to the movies. We had a nice time, and he asked me to come to the church today, which I did."

"Did you now? How was the sermon?"

"Real good. He's got brains, no doubt about it."

"You like him?"

"Yes, I like him, but that's it. What about you, Sally, are you dating anyone in particular?"

Sally was always so busy asking other people questions, she hardly ever got asked any herself. She looked quite pleased.

"Well, since you ask, I am."

"Do tell."

"This is gonna sound funny, but I'm dating Paul Allison."

"Your husband's brother?"

"Yes, that Paul Allison," she said, shaking her head in amazement at her own folly.

"You take my breath away." Paul Allison was a policeman, a detective about ten years older than Arthur—not much liked by Arthur or Lynn, if I remembered correctly. Paul was a loner, a man never married who did not join in the police force camaraderie with much gusto. He had thinning brown hair, broad shoulders, sharp blue eyes, and a suggestion of a gut. I had seen him at many parties I'd attended while I dated Arthur, but I'd never seen him with Sally.

"How long has this been going on?" I asked.

"About five months. We were at Arthur and Lynn's wedding, I tried to catch you then, but you left the church before I could. I didn't see you at the reception?"

"I had the worst headache, I thought I was starting the flu. I just went on home."

"Oh, it was just another wedding reception. Jack Burns had too much to drink and wanted to arrest one of the waiters he remembered having brought in before on drug charges."

I was even more glad I'd missed it now.

"How's Perry?" I asked reluctantly, after a pause. I was sorry to bring poor, sick Perry up, but courtesy demanded it.

"Thanks for asking," she said. "So many people don't even want to, because he's mentally sick instead of having cancer or something. But I do want people to ask, and I go see him every week. I don't want people to forget he's alive. Really, Roe, people act like Perry's dead because he's mentally ill.''

"I'm sorry, Sally.''

"Well, I do appreciate your asking. He's better, but he's not ready to get out yet. Maybe in two more months. Paul's been going with me to see Perry the past three or four times.''

"He must really love you, Sally,'' I said from my heart.

"You know,'' she said, and her face brightened, "I really think he does! Bring your plate over, I think everything's ready.''

We served ourselves from the stove, which was fine with me. Back at the table, we buttered our biscuits and said our little prayer, and dug in like we were starving.

"I guess,'' I began after I had told Sally how good everything was, "that you want to hear about Jane's house.''

"Am I as transparent as all that? Well, I did hear something, you know how gossip gets around, and I thought you would rather me ask you and get it straight than let all this talk around town get out of hand.''

"You know, you're right. I would rather you get it right and get it out on the gossip circuits. I wonder who's started the talk?''

"Uh, well . . .''

"Parnell and Leah Engle," I guessed suddenly.

"Right the first time."

"Okay, Sally. I am going to give you a gossip exclusive. There's no way this could be a story in the paper, but you see everyone in town, and you can give them the straight scoop from the horse's mouth."

"I am all ears," Sally said with a perfectly straight face.

So I told her an amended and edited account. Leaving out the cash amount, of course.

"Her savings, too?" Sally said enviously. "Oh, you lucky duck. And it's a lot?"

Glee rolled over me suddenly as it did every now and then when I forgot the skull and remembered the money. I nodded with a canary-full grin.

Sally closed her eyes in contemplation of the joy of having a lot of money all of a sudden.

"That's great," she said dreamily. "I feel good just knowing someone that's *happened* to. Like winning the lottery."

"Yeah, except Jane had to die for me to get it."

"My God, girl, she was old as the hills anyway."

"Oh, Sally, Jane wasn't so old as people go nowadays. She was in her seventies."

"That is plenty old. I won't last so long."

"I hope you do," I said mildly. "I want you to make me some more biscuits sometimes."

We talked some more about Paul Allison, which seemed to make Sally quite happy. Then I asked her about Macon Turner, her boss.

"I understand he's seeing my new maybe-neighbor, Carey Osland," I said casually.

"They are hot and heavy and have been," Sally said, with a wise nod. "That Carey is really appealing to the opposite sex. She has had quite a dating—and marriage—history."

I understood Sally exactly. "Really?"

"Oh, yes. First she was married to Bubba Sewell, back when he was nothing, just a little lawyer right out of school. Then that fell through, and she married Mike Osland, and by golly one night he goes out to get diapers and never comes home. Everyone felt so sorry for her when her husband left, and, having been in something of the same position, I did feel for her. But at the same time, I think he might have had some reason to take off."

My attention sharpened. A number of instant scenarios ran through my head. Carey's husband kills Carey's lover, then flees. The lover could have been Mark Kaplan, the Rideouts' vanished tenant, or some unknown. Or maybe Mike Osland could be the skull, reduced to that state by Carey's lover or Carey.

"But she has a little girl at home," I said in the interest of fairness.

"Wonder what she tells that little girl when she has overnight company?" Sally helped herself to more roast.

I disliked this turn of the conversation. "Well, she was very nice to me when she came over to welcome me to the neighborhood," I stated, flatly enough to end that line of conversation. Sally shot me a look and asked if I wanted more roast.

"No thanks," I said, giving a sigh of repletion. "That was so good."

"Macon really has been more agreeable at the office since he began dating Carey," Sally said abruptly. "He started seeing her after his son went away, and it just helped him deal with it a lot. Maybe Carey having somebody leave her, she was able to help Macon out."

"What son?" I didn't remember Mother mentioning any son during the time she'd dated Macon.

"He has a boy in his late teens or early twenties by now, I guess. Macon moved here after he got divorced, and the boy moved here with him, maybe seven years ago now. After a few months, the boy—his name was Edward, I think—anyway, he decided he was just going to take some savings his mother had given him and take off. He told Macon he was going to India or some such place, to contemplate or buy drugs or something. Some crazy thing. Of course, Macon was real depressed, but he couldn't stop him. The boy wrote for a while, or called, once a month...but then he stopped. And Macon hasn't seen hide nor hair of that child since then.''

"That's terrible," I said, horrified. "Wonder what happened to the boy?"

Sally shook her head pessimistically. "No telling what could happen to him wandering by himself in a country where he didn't even speak the language."

Poor Macon. "Did he go over there?"

"He talked about it for a while, but when he wrote the State Department they advised him against it. He didn't even know where Edward had been when he disappeared.... Edward could have wandered anywhere after he wrote the last letter Macon got. I remember someone from the embassy there went to the last place Edward wrote from and, according to what they told Macon, it was sort of a dive with lots of Europeans coming and going, and no one there remembered Edward, or at least that's what they were saying."

"That's awful, Sally."

"Sure is. I think Perry being in the mental hospital is better than that, I really do. At least I know where he is!"

Incontrovertible truth.

I stared into my beer bottle. Now I'd heard of one more missing person. Was a part of Edward

Turner's last remains in my mother's pink blanket bag? Since Macon told everyone he'd heard from the boy since Edward had left, Macon would have to be the guilty one. That sounded like the end of a soap opera. "Tune in tomorrow for the next installment," I murmured.

"It is like a soap," Sally agreed. "But tragic."

I began my going-away noises. The food had been great, the company at least interesting and sometimes actually fun. Sally and I parted this time fairly pleased with each other.

AFTER I LEFT SALLY'S I remembered I had to check on Madeleine. I stopped at a grocery and got some cat food and another bag of cat litter. Then I realized this looked like permanency, rather than a two-week stay while the Engles vacationed in South Carolina.

I seemed to have a pet.

I was actually looking forward to seeing the animal.

I unlocked the kitchen door at Jane's with my free hand, the other one being occupied in holding the bags from the grocery. "Madeleine?" I called. No golden purring dictator came to meet me. "Madeleine?" I said less certainly.

Could she have gotten out? The backyard door was locked, the windows still shut. I looked in the guest bedroom, since the break-in had occurred there, but the new window was still intact.

"Kitty?" I said forlornly. And then it seemed to me I heard a noise. Dreading I don't know what, I inched into Jane's bedroom. I heard the strange mew again. Had someone hurt the cat? I began shaking, I was so sure I would find a horror. I'd left the door to Jane's closet ajar, and I could tell the sound was coming from there. I pulled the door open wide, with my breath sucked in and my teeth clenched tight.

Madeleine, apparently intact, was curled up on Jane's old bathrobe, which had fallen to the bottom of the closet when I was packing clothes. She was lying on her side, her muscles rippling as she strained.

Madeleine was having kittens.

"OH HELL," I SAID. "Oh—hell hell hell." I slumped on the bed despondently. Madeleine spared me a golden glare and went back to work. "Why me, Lord?" I asked self-pityingly. Though I had to concede it looked like Madeleine would be saying the same thing if she could. Actually, this was rather interesting. Would Madeleine mind if I watched? Apparently not, because she didn't hiss or claw at me when I sat on the floor just outside the closet and kept her company.

Of course Parnell Engle had been fully aware of Madeleine's impending motherhood, hence his merriment when I'd told him Madeleine could stay with me.

I pondered that for a few seconds, trying to decide if Parnell and I were even now. Maybe so, for Madeleine had had three kittens already, and there seemed to be more on the way.

I kept telling myself this was the miracle of birth. It sure was messy. Madeleine had my complete sympathy. She gave a final heave, and out popped another tiny, slimy kitten. I hoped two things: that this was the last kitten and that Madeleine didn't run into any difficulties, because I was the last person in the world who could offer her any help. After a few minutes, I began to think both my hopes had been fulfilled. Madeleine cleaned the little things, and all four lay there, occasionally making tiny movements, eyes shut, about as defenseless as anything could be.

Madeleine looked at me with the weary superiority of someone who has bravely undergone a major milestone. I wondered if she were thirsty; I got her water bowl and put it near her, and her food bowl, too. She got up after a moment and took a drink but didn't seem too interested in her food. She settled back down with her babies and looked perfectly all right, so I left her and went to sit in the living room. I stared at the bookshelves and wondered what in hell I would do with four kittens. On a shelf separate from those holding all the fictional and nonfictional murders, I saw several books about cats. Maybe that was what I should dip into next.

Right above the cat shelf was Jane's collection of books about Madeleine Smith, the Scottish poisoner, Jane's favorite. All of us former members of Real Murders had a favorite or two. My mother's new husband was a Lizzie Borden expert. I tended to favor Jack the Ripper, though I had by no means attained the status of Ripperologist.

But Jane Engle had always been a Madeleine Smith buff. Madeleine had been released after her trial after receiving the Scottish verdict "Not Proven," wonderfully accurate. She had almost certainly poisoned her perfidious former lover, a clerk, so she could marry into her own respectable upper-middle-class milieu without the clerk's revealing their physical intimacy. Poison was a curiously secret kind of revenge; the hapless L'Angelier had deceived himself that he was dealing with an average girl of the time, though the ardency of her physical expressions of love should have proved to him that Madeleine had a deep vein of passion. That passion extended to keeping her name clean and her reputation intact. L'Angelier threatened to send Madeleine's explicit love letters to her father.

Madeleine pretended to effect a reconciliation, then slipped arsenic into L'Angelier's cup of chocolate.

For lack of anything better to do, I pulled out one of the Smith books and began to flip through it. It fell open right away. There was a yellow Post-it note stuck to the top of the page.

It said, in Jane's handwriting, *I didn't do it.*

SEVEN

I DIDN'T DO IT.

The first thing I felt was overwhelming relief. Jane, who had left me so much, had not left me holding the bag, so to speak, on a murder she herself had committed.

She had left me in the position of concealing the murder someone else had committed, a murder Jane also had concealed, for reasons I could not fathom.

I had believed the only question I had to answer was Whose skull? Now I had also to find out who put the hole in that skull.

Was my situation really any better? No, I decided after some consideration. My conscience weighed perhaps an ounce less. The question of going to the police took on a different slant now that I would not be accusing Jane of murder by taking in the skull. But she'd had something to do with it. Oh, what a mess!

Not for the first (or the last) time, I wished I could have five minutes' conversation with Jane Engle, my benefactress and my burden. I tried to think of the money, to cheer myself up; I reminded myself that the will was a little closer to probate now, I'd be able to actually spend some without consulting Bubba Sewell beforehand.

And to tell you the truth, I still felt excellent about that money. I had read so many mysteries in which the private detective had sent back his retainer check because the payer was immoral or the job he was hired to do turned out to be against his code of honor. Jane wanted me to have that money to have fun with, and she wanted me to remember her. Well, here I was remembering every single day, by golly, and I certainly intended to have fun. In the meantime, I had a problem to solve.

It seemed to me that Bubba knew something about this. Could I retain him as my lawyer and ask him what to do? Wouldn't attorney-client privilege cover my admission I'd located and rehidden the skull? Or would Bubba, as an officer of the court, be obliged to disclose my little lapse? I'd read a lot of mysteries that had probably contained this information, but now they all ran together in my head. The laws probably varied from state to state, too.

I could tell Aubrey, surely? Would he be obligated to tell the police? Would he have any practical advice to offer? I was pretty confident I knew what his moral advice would be; the skull should go into the police station now, today, pronto. I was concealing the death of someone who had been dead and missing for over three years, at a minimum. Someone, somewhere, needed to know this person had died. What if this was Macon Turner's son? Macon had been wanting to know the whereabouts of his son for a long time, had been searching for him; if there was even a faint chance his son's letters to him had been forged, it was inhumane to keep this knowledge from Macon.

Unless Macon had caused the hole in the skull.

Carey Osland had believed all these years her husband had walked out on her. She should know he had been prevented from returning home with those diapers.

Unless Carey herself had prevented him.

Marcia and Torrance Rideout needed to know their tenant had not voluntarily skipped out on his rent.

Unless they themselves had canceled his lease.

I jumped to my feet and went into the kitchen to fix myself—something. Anything. Of course, all that was there was canned stuff and unopened packages. I ended up with a jar of peanut butter and a spoon. I stuck the spoon in the jar and stood at the counter licking the peanut butter off.

Murderers needed to be exposed, truth needed to see the light of day. Et cetera. Then I had another thought: whoever had broken into this house, searching for the skull, had been the murderer.

I shivered. Not nice to think.

And even now, that little thought trickled onward, that murderer was wondering if I'd found the skull yet, what I'd do with it.

"This is bad," I muttered. "Really, really bad."

That was constructive thinking.

Start at ground zero.

Okay. Jane had seen a murder, or maybe someone burying a body. For her to get the skull, she had to know the body was there, right? Jane literally knew where the bodies were buried. I actually caught myself smiling at my little joke.

Why would she not tell the police immediately?

No answer.

Why would she take the skull?

No answer.

Why would anyone pick Jane's demise as the time to look for the skull, when she'd obviously had it for years?

Possible answer: the murderer did not know for sure that Jane was the person who had the skull.

I imagined someone who had committed a terrible crime in the throes of who knew what passion or pressure. After hiding the body somewhere, suddenly this murderer finds that the skull is gone, the skull with its telltale hole, the skull with its identifiable teeth. Someone has taken the trouble to dig it up and take it away and the killer doesn't know who.

How horrible. I could almost pity the murderer. What fear, what terror, what dreadful uncertainty.

I shook myself. I should be feeling sorry for The Skull, as I thought of it.

Where could Jane have seen a murder?

Her own backyard. She had had to know where the body was buried exactly; she had had to have leisure to dig without interruption or discovery, presumably; she could not have carted a skull any distance. My reasoning of a few days before was still valid, whether or not Jane was the murderer. The murder had happened on this street, in one of these houses, somewhere where Jane could see it.

So I went out in the backyard and looked.

I found myself staring at the two cement benches flanking the birdbath. Jane had been fond of sitting there in the evenings, I recalled her saying. Sometimes the birds had perched on the bath while she sat there, she could sit so still, she had told me proudly. I did wonder if Madeleine had been outside with Jane enjoying this, and dismissed the thought as unworthy. Jane had been many things—I seemed to be finding more and more things she'd been every day—but she hadn't been an out-and-out sadist.

I sat on one of the cement benches with my back to Carey Osland's house. I could see almost all the Rideouts' sun deck clearly, of course: no Marcia in red there today. I could see their old garden plot and some clear lawn. The very rear of their yard was obscured by the bushes in my own yard. Beyond the Rideouts' I could discern one little section of Macon Turner's, which had lots of large bushes and rather high grass. I would have to come out here at night, I thought, to find if I could see through the windows of any of these houses.

It was hot, and I was full of roast beef and peanut butter. I slid into a trance, mentally moving people around their backyards, in various murderous postures.

"What you doing?" asked a voice behind me curiously.

I gasped and jumped.

A little girl stood behind me. She was maybe seven or eight or even a little older, and she was wearing shorts and a pink T-shirt. She had chin-length, wavy, dark hair and big dark eyes and glasses.

"I'm sitting," I said tensely. "What are you doing?"

"My mom sent me over to ask you if you could come drink some coffee with her."

"Who's your mom?"

Now that was funny, someone not knowing who her mom was.

"Carey Osland." She giggled. "In that house right there," she pointed, obviously believing she was dealing with a mentally deficient person.

The Osland backyard was almost bare of bushes or any concealment at all. There was a swing set and a sandbox; I could see the street to the other side of the house easily.

This was the child who had needed diapers the night her father left the house and never returned.

"Yes, I'll come," I said. "What's your name?"

"Linda. Well, come on."

So I followed Linda Osland over to her mother's house, wondering what Carey had to say.

CAREY, I DECIDED after a while, had just been being hospitable.

She'd gone the afternoon before to pick up Linda from camp, had spent Sunday morning washing Linda's shorts and shirts, which had been indescribably filthy, had listened to all Linda's camp stories, and now was ready for some adult companionship. Macon, she told me, was out playing golf at the country club. She said it like she had a right to know his whereabouts at all times and like other people should realize that. So, if their relationship had had its clandestine moments, it was moving out into the open. I noticed that she didn't say anything about their getting married, and didn't hint that was in the future.

Maybe they were happy just like they were.

It would be a great thing, not to want to get married. I sighed, I hoped imperceptibly, and asked Carey about Jane.

"I feel myself wanting to get to know her better now," I said, with a what-can-you-do? shrug.

"Well, Jane was a different kettle of fish," Carey said, with a lift of her dark brows.

"She was an old meanie," Linda said suddenly. She'd been sitting at the table cutting out paper doll clothes.

"Linda," her mother admonished, without any real scolding in her voice.

"Well, remember, Mama, how mad she got at Burger King!"

I tried to look politely baffled.

Carey's pretty, round face looked a little peeved for just a second. "More coffee?" she asked.

"Yes, thanks," I said, to gain more time before I had to go.

Carey poured and showed no sign of explaining Linda's little remark.

"Jane was a difficult neighbor?" I asked tentatively.

"Oh." Carey sighed with pursed lips. "I wish Linda hadn't brought that up. Honey, you got to learn to forget unpleasant things and old fights, it doesn't pay to remember stuff like that."

Linda nodded obediently and went back to her scissors.

"Burger King was our dog; Linda named him of course," Carey explained reluctantly. "We didn't keep him on a leash, I know we should have, and of course our backyard isn't fenced in . . ."

I nodded encouragingly.

"Naturally, he eventually got run over, I'm ashamed of us even having an outside dog without having a fence," Carey confessed, shaking her head at her own negligence. "But Linda did want a pet, and she's allergic to cats."

"I sneeze and my eyes get red," Linda explained.

"Yes, honey. Of course, we had the dog when Jane had just gotten her cat, and of course Burger King chased Madeleine every time Jane let her out, which wasn't too often, but every now and then . . ." Carey lost her thread.

"The dog treed the cat?" I suggested helpfully.

"Oh yes, and barked and barked," Carey said ruefully. "It was a mess. And Jane got so mad about it."

"She said she would call the pound," Linda chimed in. "Because there's a leash law and we were breaking it."

"Well, honey, she was right," Carey said. "We were."

"She didn't have to be so mean about it," Linda insisted.

"She was a little shirty," Carey said confidentially to me. "I mean, I know I was at fault, but she really went off the deep end."

"Oh dear," I murmured.

"I'm surprised Linda remembers any of this because it was a long time ago. Years, I guess."

"So did Jane end up calling the animal control people?"

"No, no. Poor Burger got hit by a car over on Faith, right here to the side of the house, very soon after that. So now we have Waldo here"—and the tip of her slipper poked the dachshund affectionately—"and we walk him three or four times a day. It's not much of a life for him, but it's the best we can do."

Waldo snored contentedly.

"Speaking of Madeleine, she came home," I told Carey.

"She did! I thought Parnell and Leah picked her up from the vet's where she'd been boarded while Jane was sick?"

"Well, they did, but Madeleine wanted to be at her own house. As it turns out, she was expecting."

Linda and Carey both exclaimed over that, and I regretted telling them after a moment, because of course Linda wanted to see the little kitties and her mother did not want the child to cough and weep all afternoon.

"I'm sorry, Carey," I said as I took my leave.

"Don't worry about it," Carey insisted, though I am sure she wished I had kept my mouth shut. "It's just one of those things Linda has to learn to live with. I sure hope someday I can afford to fence the backyard, I'll get her a Scottie puppie, I swear I will. A friend of mine raises them, and those are the cutest puppies in the world. Like little walking shoe brushes."

I considered the cute factor of walking shoe brushes as I went through Carey's backyard to my own. Carey's yard was so open to view it was hard to imagine where a body could have been buried on her property, but I couldn't exclude Carey either; her yard might not have been so bare a few years before.

I could be rid of all this by getting in my car and driving to the police station, I reminded myself. And for a moment I was powerfully tempted.

And I'll tell you what stopped me: not loyalty to Jane, not keeping faith with the dead; nothing so noble. It was my fear of Sergeant Jack Burns, the terrifying head of the detectives. The sergeant, I had observed in my previous contacts with him, burned for truth the way other men burn for a promotion or a night with Michelle Pfeiffer.

He wouldn't be happy with me.

He would want to nail me to the wall.

I would keep the skull a secret a little longer.

Maybe somehow I could wriggle out of this with a clear conscience. That didn't seem possible at this moment, but then it hadn't seemed possible someone would die and leave me a fortune, either.

I went in to check on Madeleine. She was nursing her kittens and looking smug and tired at the same time. I refilled her water bowl. I started to move her litter box into the room with her, but then I reconsidered. Best to leave it in the place she was used to going.

"Just think," I told the cat, "a week ago, I had no idea that soon I'd have a cat, four kittens, a house, five hundred and fifty thousand dollars, and a skull. I didn't know what I was missing."

The doorbell rang.

I jumped maybe a mile. Thanks to Jane's cryptic note, I now knew I had something to fear.

"Be back in a minute, Madeleine," I said, to reassure myself rather than the cat.

This time, instead of opening the door, I looked through Jane's spyhole. When I saw lots of black, I knew my caller was Aubrey. I was smiling as I opened the door.

"Come in."

"I just thought I'd drop by and see the new house," he said hesitantly. "Is that okay?"

"Sure. I just found out today I have kittens, come see them."

And I led Aubrey into the bedroom, telling him Madeleine's saga as we went.

The proximity of the bed startled him a little, but the kittens entranced him.

"Want one?" I asked. "It occurs to me I'll have to find homes for all of them in a few weeks. I'll have to call a vet and find out when they can be separated from her. And when I can have her neutered."

"You're not going to take her back to Jane's cousin?" Aubrey asked, looking a little amused.

"No," I said without even thinking about it. "I'll see how I like living with a pet. She seems pretty attached to this house."

"Maybe I will take one," Aubrey said thoughtfully. "My little house can get lonely. Having a cat to come home to might be pretty nice. I do get asked out a lot. That's where I've been since church, as a matter of fact; a family in the church asked me to their home for lunch."

"I bet it wasn't as good as my lunch." I told him about Sally's roast beef, and he said he'd had turkey, and we ended up sitting by the kittens talking about food for a while. He didn't cook for himself much, either.

And the doorbell rang.

We had been getting along so cozily, I had to resist an impulse to say something very nasty.

I left him in the bedroom staring at the kittens, all asleep and tiny, while I scrambled into the living room and opened the door.

Marcia Rideout, wide awake and gorgeous in white cotton shorts and a bright red camp shirt, smiled back at me. She certainly wasn't drunk now; she was alert and cheerful.

"Good to see you again," she said with a smile.

I marveled again at her perfect grooming. Her lipstick was almost professionally applied, her eye shadow subtle but noticeable, her hair evenly golden and smoothly combed into a page boy. Her legs were hairless and beautifully brown. Even her white tennis shoes were spotless.

"Hi, Marcia," I said quickly, having become aware I was staring at her like a guppy.

"I'll just take a minute of your time," she promised. She handed me a little envelope. "Torrance and I just want to give a little party on our sun deck this Wednesday to welcome you into the neighborhood."

"Oh, but I—" I began to protest.

"No no, now. We wanted to have a little cookout anyway, but your inheriting the house just makes a good excuse. And we have new neighbors across the street, too, they're going to come. We'll all get to know each other. I know this is short notice, but Torrance has to travel this Friday and won't be back until late on Saturday." Marcia seemed like a different person from the indolent drunk I'd met a few days before. The prospect of entertaining seemed to bring her to life.

How could I refuse? The idea of being honored at the same party with Lynn and Arthur was less than thrilling, but refusal would be unthinkable, too.

"Do bring a date if you want, or just come on your own," Marcia said.

"You really won't mind if I bring someone?"

"Please do! One more won't make a bit of difference. Got anyone in mind?" Marcia asked, her brows arched coyly.

"Yes," I said with a smile, and said no more. I was just hoping with all my might that Aubrey would not choose this moment to emerge from the bedroom. I could picture Marcia's eyebrows flying clean off her face.

"Oh," Marcia said, obviously a little taken aback by my marked lack of explanation. "Yes, that'll be fine. Just come as you are, we won't be fancy, that's not Torrance and me!"

Marcia seemed very fancy indeed to me.

"Can I bring anything?"

"Just yourself," Marcia responded, as I'd expected. I realized that the party preparations would keep her excited and happy for the next three days.

"I'll see you then," she called as she bounced down the steps and started back over to her house.

I took the little invitation with me when I went back to Aubrey.

"Could you go to this with me?" I asked, handing it to him. I thought if he turned me down I was going to be horribly embarrassed, but I had no one else to ask, and if I was going to a party with Arthur and Lynn present, I was damn sure going to have a date.

He pulled the invitation out and read it. It had a chef on the front wearing a barbecue apron and holding a long fork. "Something good is on the grill!" exclaimed the print. When you opened it, it said, ". . . and you can share it with us on *Wednesday, 7:00* at *Marcia and Torrance's* house. See you then!"

"A little on the hearty side," I said, as neutrally as I could. I didn't want to seem uncharitable.

"I'm sure I can, but let me check." Aubrey pulled a little black notebook out of his pocket. "The liturgical calendar," he explained. "I think every Episcopalian priest carries one of these." He flipped through the pages, then beamed up at me. "Sure, I can go." I blew out a sigh of sheer relief. Aubrey produced a little pencil in disgraceful shape and wrote in the time and address, and, to my amusement, "Pick up Aurora." Would he forget me otherwise?

Stuffing the book back into his pocket, he got to his feet and told me he'd better be going. "I have youth group in an hour,'' he said, checking his watch.

"What do you do with them?'' I asked as I walked him to the door.

"Try to make them feel okay about not being Baptists and having a big recreation center to go to, mostly. We go in with the Lutherans and the Presbyterians, taking turns to have the young people on Sunday evening. And it's my church's turn.''

At least it was too early in our relationship for me to feel at all obliged to take part in that.

Aubrey opened the door to leave, then seemed to remember something he'd forgotten. He bent over to give me a kiss, his arm loosely around my shoulders. There was no doubt this time about the jolt I felt clear down to the soles of my feet. When he straightened up, he looked a little energized himself.

"Well!'' he said breathless. "I'll give you a call this week, and I look forward to Wednesday night.''

"Me, too,'' I said with a smile, and saw past his shoulder the curtains in the house across the way stir.

Ha! I thought maturely, as I shut the door behind Aubrey.

EIGHT

MONDAY TURNED OUT TO BE a much busier day than I'd expected. When I went in to work to put in what I thought would be four hours, I found that one of the other librarians had caught a summer cold ("The worst kind," all the other librarians said wisely, shaking their heads. I thought any cold was the worst kind). The head of the library, Sam Clerrick, asked if I'd put in eight hours instead, and after a little hesitation I agreed. I felt very gracious, because now I had it within my financial power (well, almost within my financial power) to quit my job completely. There's nothing like patting yourself on the back to give you energy; I worked happily all morning, reading to a circle of preschoolers and answering questions.

I did feel justified in taking a few extra minutes on my coffee break to call the phone company and ask them if the number I had at the town house could also be the number for Jane's house, at least for a while. Even if that wasn't possible, I wanted Jane's phone hooked back up. To my pleasure, it was possible to get my number to ring at Jane's, and I was assured it would be operational within the next couple of days.

As I was hanging up, Lillian Schmidt lumbered in. Lillian is one of those disagreeable people who yet have some redeeming qualities, so that you can't write them off entirely—but you sure wish you could. Furthermore, I worked with Lillian, so it was in my interest to keep peace with her. Lillian was narrow-minded and gossipy, but fair; she was a devoted wife and mother, but talked about her husband and daughter until you wanted them to be swallowed up in an earthquake; she knew her job and did it competently, but with so much groaning and complaining about minute details that you wanted to smack her. Reacting to Lillian, I sounded like a wild-eyed Communist, an incurable Polly-anna, and a free-sex advocate.

"It's so hot outside, I feel like I need another shower," she said by way of greeting. Her fore-head was beaded with perspiration. She pulled a tissue from the box on the coffee table and dabbed at her face.

"I hear you had a windfall," she continued, tossing the tissue into the trash and missing. With a deep sigh, Lillian laboriously bent over to re-trieve it. But her eyes flicked up to take in my re-action.

"Yes," I said with a bright smile.

Lillian waited for me to elaborate. She eyed me wryly when I didn't say anything. "I didn't know you and Jane Engle were such good friends."

I considered several possible responses, smiling all the while. "We were friends."

Lillian shook her head slowly. "I was a friend of Jane's, too, but she didn't leave me any house."

What could I say to that? I shrugged. If Jane and Lillian had had any special personal relationship, I certainly couldn't recall it.

"Did you know," Lillian continued, switching to another track, "that Bubba Sewell is going to run for state representative in the fall?"

"Is he really." It wasn't a question.

Lillian saw that she'd made an impression. "Yes, his secretary is my sister-in-law, so she told me even before the announcement, which is tomorrow. I knew you'd be interested since I saw you talking to him at Jane's funeral. He's trying to get his house in order, so to speak, so he doesn't want even a whiff of anything funny that might be dug up during the campaign. He's going to be running against Carl Underwood, and Carl's had that seat for three terms."

Lillian had gotten to give me information I hadn't possessed, and that had made her happy. After a couple more complaints about the school system's insensitivity to her daughter's allergies, she stumped off to actually do some work.

I remained seated on the hard chair in the tiny coffee-break room, thinking hard about Bubba Sewell. No wonder he hadn't wanted to know what was fishy in Jane's house! No wonder he had catered to her so extensively. It was good word of mouth for him, that he would go to such lengths for his elderly client, especially since he wasn't gaining anything from her will—except a fat fee for handling it.

If I told Bubba Sewell about the skull he'd hate me for the rest of his life. And he was Carey Osland's first husband; maybe somehow he was involved in the disappearance of Carey's second husband?

As I washed my mug in the little sink and set it in the drainer, I dismissed any urge I'd ever felt to confide in the lawyer. He was running for office; he was ambitious; he couldn't be trusted. A pretty grim summation for someone who might be my elected representative in the statehouse. I sighed, and started for the check-in desk to shelve the returned books.

ON MY LUNCH HOUR, I ran over to the house on Honor to let the cat out and check on the kittens. I picked up a hamburger and drink at a drive-through.

When I turned off Faith I saw a city work crew cleaning the honeysuckle and poison ivy from around the DEAD END sign at the end of the street. It would take them hours. Vines and weeds had taken over the little area and had obviously been thriving for years, twining around the sign itself and then attaching to the rear fence of the house backing onto the end of our street. The city truck was parked right in the middle of the road down by Macon Turner's house.

For the first time since I'd inherited Jane's house, I saw the newspaper editor himself, perhaps also returning to his home for lunch. Macon's thinning, brownish-gray hair was long and combed across the top of his head to give his scalp some coverage. He had an intelligent face, thin lipped and sharp, and wore suits that always seemed to need to go to the cleaners; in fact, Macon always gave the impression that he did not know how to take care of himself. His hair always needed trimming, his clothes needed ironing, he usually seemed tired, and he was always one step behind his schedule. He called to me now as he pulled letters out of his mailbox, giving me a smile that held a heavy dose of charm. Macon was the only man my mother had ever dated that I personally found attractive.

I waited, standing in the driveway with my little paper bag of lunch in one hand and my house keys in the other, while Macon walked over. His tie was crooked, and he was carrying his suit coat, a lightweight khaki, almost dragging the ground. I wondered if Carey Osland, whose house was not exactly a model of neatness, realized what she was taking on.

"Good to see you, Roe! How's your mother and her new husband?" Macon called before he was quite close enough. The cleanup crew, two young black men being watched by an older one, turned their heads to cast us a glance.

It was one of those moments that you always remember for no apparent reason. It was dreadfully hot, the sun brilliant in a cloudless sky. The three workmen had huge, dark stains on their shirts, and one of the younger men had a red bandanna over his head. The ancient city dump truck was painted dark orange. Condensation from the cup containing my soft drink was making a wet blotch on the paper bag; I worried that the bag would break. I was feeling glad to see Macon, but also impatient to get inside the cool house and eat lunch and check on Madeleine's brood. I felt a trickle of sweat start up under my green-and-white-striped dress, felt it roll its ticklish way down under my belt to my hips. I looped my purse strap over my shoulder so I could have a free hand to hold up my hair in the vain hope of catching a breeze across my neck; I hadn't had time to braid my hair that morning. I looked down at a crack in the driveway and wondered how to get it repaired. Weeds were growing through in unattractive abundance.

I was just thinking that I was glad Mother had married John Queensland, whom I found worthy but often boring, rather than Macon, whose face was made disturbingly attractive by his intelligence, when one of the workmen let out a yell. It hung in the thick, hot air; all three men froze. Macon's head turned in midstride, and he paused as his foot hit the ground. All movement seemed to become deliberate. I was acutely aware of turning my head slightly, the better to see what the man with the red bandanna was lifting off the ground. The contrast of his black hand against the white bone was riveting.

"God almighty! It's a dead man!" bellowed the other worker, and the slow motion speeded up into a sequence too swift for me to replay afterward.

I DECIDED THAT DAY that the dead person could not be Macon Turner's son; or, at least if it was, Edward had not been killed by Macon. Macon's face never showed the slightest hint that this find might have a personal slant. He was excited and interested and almost broke his door down to get in to call the police.

Lynn came out of her house when the police car appeared. She looked pale and miserable. Her belly preceded her like a tugboat pulling her along.

"What's the fuss?" she asked, nodding toward the workmen, who were reliving their find complete with quotes and gestures while the patrolman peered down into the thick weeds and vines choking the base of the sign.

"A skeleton, I think," I said cautiously. Though I was sure it was not a *complete* skeleton.

Lynn looked unmoved. "I bet it turns out to be a Great Dane or some other big dog. Maybe even some cow bones or deer bones left over from some home butchering."

"Could be," I said. I looked up at Lynn, whose hand was absently massaging her bulging belly. "How are you doing?"

"I feel like..." She paused to think. "I feel like if I bent over, the baby's so low I could shake hands with it."

"Oo," I said. I squinched up my face trying to imagine it.

"You've never been pregnant," Lynn said, a member of a club I'd never belonged to. "It's not as easy as you might think, considering women have done it for millions of years." Right now, Lynn was a lot more interested in her own body than in the body at the end of the road.

"So you're not working now?" I asked, keeping one eye cocked at the patrolman, who was now using his radio. The workmen had calmed down and moved into the shade of a tree in Macon's front yard. Macon disappeared into his house, popping back out with a camera and notepad.

"No. My doctor told me I had to take off work and keep my feet up for as long each day as I can. Since we got most of the boxes unpacked and the nursery is ready, I just do house things about two hours each day, and the rest of the time," she told me gloomily, "I just wait."

This was so—un-Lynn.

"Are you excited?" I asked hesitantly.

"I'm too uncomfortable to be excited. Besides, Arthur is excited enough for both of us."

I found that hard to picture.

"You don't mind anymore, do you?" Lynn asked suddenly.

"No."

"You dating anyone else?"

"Sort of. But I just stopped minding."

Luckily Lynn stopped there, because I simply would not say anything more about it.

"Do you think you'll keep the house?"

"I have no idea." I almost asked Lynn if it would bother her if I did, then I realized I didn't want to know the answer.

"Are you going to that party?" Lynn asked after a moment.

"Yes."

"We will too, I guess, though I'm not much in partying shape. That Marcia Rideout looked at me like she'd never seen a pregnant woman when she came over to meet me and leave the invitation. She made me feel like the Goodyear blimp and an un-made bed all at once.''

I could see how that would be, given Marcia's aggressively good grooming.

"I better go check on the kittens," I told Lynn. The situation down at the end of the street was static. The patrolman leaned against his car, wait-ing for someone else to show up, apparently. Ma-con was standing at the end of the pavement looking down at the bones. The workmen were smoking and drinking RC Colas.

"Oh, you have kittens? Can I see?" For the first time, Lynn looked animated.

"Sure," I said with some surprise. Then I real-ized Lynn was in the mood to see baby anything.

The kittens were more active today. They tum-bled over one another, their eyes still not open, and Madeleine surveyed them with queenly pride. One was coal black, the others marmalade and white like their mother. Soon their energy ran out and they began to nurse, dropping off into sleep di-rectly after. Lynn had carefully lowered herself to the floor and watched silently, her face unread-able. I went into the kitchen to replenish Made-leine's water and food, and I changed the litter box while I was at it. After I washed my hands and had a gulp of my drink and most of my hamburger, I went back to the bedroom to find Lynn still staring.

"Did you watch them being born?" she asked.

"Yep."

"Did it look like she hurt?"

"It looked like it was work," I said carefully.

She sighed heavily. "Well, I expect that," she said, trying to sound philosophical.

"Have you gone to Lamaze?"

"Oh, yeah. We do our breathing exercises every night," she said unenthusiastically.

"You don't think they're going to work?"

"I have no idea. You know what's really scary?"

"What?"

"No one will tell you."

"Like who?"

"*Anyone.* It's the damnedest thing. I really want to know what I'm up against. So I ask my best friend, she's had two. She says, 'Oh, when you see what you get it's worth it.' That's no answer, right? So I ask someone else who didn't use any anesthesia. She says, 'Oh, you'll forget all about it when you see the baby.' That's not an answer either. And my mom was knocked out, old-style, when she had me. So she can't tell me, and she probably wouldn't. It's some kind of mom conspiracy."

I thought it over. "Well, I sure can't answer any questions, but I'd tell you the truth if I could."

"I expect," Lynn said, "that I'll be telling you, and pretty soon."

WHEN I LEFT THE HOUSE to return to the library, I saw two police cars parked in Macon Turner's driveway, and the city truck was gone. The rest of the skeleton having been found was a great relief to me. Now the police would be working on finding out who it was. Perhaps the remaining bones would be enough? If they could find out from the bones, I mentally promised The Skull I would give it a decent burial.

I was guiltily aware I was not taking any morally firm position.

That evening the doorbell rang just as I had eased off my shoes and rolled my panty hose down. I hastily yanked them off, pushed them under my chair, and stuck my bare feet into my shoes. I was a hot, wrinkled mess with a headache and a bad conscience.

Sergeant Jack Burns filled my doorway form side to side. His clothes were always heavy on polyester, and he had long Elvis sideburns, but nothing could detract from the air of menace that emanated from him in a steady stream. He was so used to projecting it that I think he might have been surprised if you had told him about it.

"May I come in?" he asked gently.

"Oh, of course," I said, backing to one side.

"I come to ask you about the bones found today on Honor Street," he said formally.

"Please come have a seat."

"Thank you, I will, I been on my old feet all day," he said in a courtly way. He let himself down on my couch, and I sat opposite him in my favorite chair.

"You just come in from work?"

"Yes, yes I did."

"But you were at Jane Engle's house on Honor Street today when the road crew found the skeleton."

"Yes, I had come there on my lunch hour to feed the cat."

He stared and waited. He was better at this than I was.

"Jane's cat. Uh—she ran away from Parnell and Leah Engle and came back home, she had kittens in the closet. In Jane's bedroom."

"You know, you sure turn up a lot for a law-abiding citizen, Miss Teagarden. We hardly seem to have any homicides in Lawrenceton without you showing up. Seems mighty strange."

"I would hardly call having inherited a house on the same street 'mighty strange,' Sergeant Burns," I said bravely.

"Well, now you think about it," he suggested in a reasonable voice. "Last year when we had those deaths, there you were. When we caught them that did it, there you were.''

About to get killed myself, I said, but only in my head, because you didn't interrupt Sergeant Jack Burns.

''Then Miss Engle dies, and here you are on the street with a skeleton in the weeds, a street with a suspicious number of reported break-ins, including one in this house you just inherited.''

''A suspicious number of break-ins? Are you saying other people on Honor besides me have reported their house being entered?''

''That's what I'm saying, Miss Teagarden.''

''And nothing taken?''

''Nothing the owner would admit to missing. Maybe the thief took some pornographic books or some other thing the homeowner would be embarrassed to report.''

''There certainly wasn't anything like that in Jane's house, I'm sure,'' I said indignantly. Just an old skull with some holes in it. ''It may be that something was missing, I wouldn't know. I only saw the house after the burglary. Ah—who else reported their houses had been broken into?''

Jack Burns actually looked surprised before he looked suspicious.

''Everyone, now. Except that old couple in the end house on the other side of the street. Now, do you know anything about the bones found to-day?"

"Oh, no. I just happened along when they were discovered. You know, I've only been in the house a few times, and I've never stayed there. I only visited Jane, over the past couple of years. Before she went into the hospital."

"I think," Jack Burns said heavily and unfairly, "this is one mystery the police department can handle, Miss Teagarden. You keep your little bitty nose out of it."

"Oh," I said furiously, "I will, Sergeant." And as I rose to show him out, my heel caught on the balled-up panty hose under my chair and dragged them out for Jack Burns's viewing.

He gave them a look of scorn, as if they'd been sleazy sexual aids, and departed with his awful majesty intact. If he had laughed, he would've been human.

NINE

I'D ONLY HAD HALF a cup of coffee the next morning when the phone rang. I'd gotten up late after an uneasy sleep. I'd dreamed the skull was under my bed and Jack Burns was sitting in a chair by the bed interrogating me while I was in my nightgown. I was sure somehow he would read my mind and bend over to look under the bed; and if he did that I was doomed. I woke up just as he was lifting the bedspread.

After I'd poured my coffee, made my toast, and retrieved my Lawrenceton *Sentinel* from the front doorstep, I settled at the kitchen table for my morning read. I'd gotten the page one lead story (SEWELL CHALLENGES INCUMBENT) skimmed and was just searching for the comics when I was interrupted.

I picked up the phone, convinced the call was bad news, so I was pleasantly surprised to here Amina's mom on the other end. As it turned out, my original premise was correct.

"Good morning, Aurora! It's Joe Nell Day."

"Hi, Miss Joe Nell. How you doing?" Amina bravely called my mother "Miss Aida."

"Just fine, thanks, honey. Listen, Amina called me last night to tell me they've moved the wedding day up."

I felt a chill of sheer dismay. Here we go again, I thought gloomily. But this was Amina's mother. I stretched my mouth into a smile so my voice would match. "Well, Miss Joe Nell, they're both old enough to know what they're doing," I said heartily.

"I sure hope so," she said from the heart. "I'd sure hate Amina to go through another divorce."

"No, not going to happen," I said, offering reassurance I didn't feel. "This is going to be the one."

"We'll pray about it," Miss Joe Nell said earnestly. "Amina's daddy is fit to be tied. We haven't even met this young man yet."

"You liked her first husband," I said. Amina would always marry someone nice. It was staying that way that was the problem. What was this guy's name? Hugh Price. "She had so many positive things to tell me about Hugh." He was positively good-looking, he was positively rich, he was positively good in bed. I hoped he wasn't positively shallow. I hoped Amina really loved him. I wasn't too concerned about him loving Amina; I took that as an easy accomplishment since I loved her.

"Well, they're both veterans of the divorce wars, so they should know what they want and don't want. Anyway, why I called you, Aurora, moving up the wedding day means you need to come in and get fitted for your bridesmaid's dress.''

"Am I the only one?'' I hoped desperately I could wear something personally becoming rather than something that was supposed to look good on five or six different females of varying builds and complexions.

"Yes,'' said Miss Joe Nell with open relief. "Amina wants you to come down and pick what you want as long as it will look good with her dress, which is mint green.''

Not white. I was kind of surprised. Since Amina had decided to send out invitations and have a larger wedding because her first one was so hole-in-the-wall, I'd felt she'd do the whole kit and caboodle. I was relieved to hear she was moderating her impulse.

"Sure, I can come in this morning,'' I said obligingly. "I don't have to work today.''

"Oh, that's just great! I'll see you then.''

This was when your mother owning a dress shop was really convenient. There was sure to be something at Great Day that would suit me. If not, Miss Joe Nell would find something.

When I went upstairs to get dressed, on impulse I turned into the back bedroom, the guest room. The only guest who'd ever slept in it had been my little half brother Phillip when he used to come spend an occasional weekend with me. Now he was all the way in California; our father and his mother had wanted to get him as far away from me and Lawrenceton as possible, so he wouldn't have to remember what had happened to him here. While he was staying with me.

I fought off drearily familiar feelings of guilt and pain, and flung open the closet door. In this closet I kept the things I wasn't wearing currently, heavy winter coats, my few cocktail and evening dresses . . . and my bridesmaid dresses. There were four of them: a lavender ruffled horror from Sally Saxby's wedding, Linda Erhardt's floral chiffon, a red velvet with white "fur" trim from my college roommate's Christmas "nuptials," and a somewhat better pink sheath from Franny Vargas's spring marriage. The lavender had made me look as if I'd been bushwhacked by a Barbie doll, the floral chiffon was not bad but in blondes' colors, the red velvet had made me look like Dolly Parton in the chest but otherwise we'd all looked like Santa's helpers, and the pink sheath I'd had cut to knee length and had actually worn to some parties over the years.

I'd worn jeans to Amina's first, runaway wedding.

That had been the most useful bridesmaid's outfit of all.

Now that I had worked myself into an absolutely great mood, what with thinking of Phillip and reviewing my history as a bridesmaid, I decided I'd better get myself in gear and go do things.

What did I need to do besides go by Great Day?

I had to go check on Madeleine and the kittens. I had to go by Mother's office; she'd asked me to on the message left on my machine, and I hadn't done it yet. I felt an urge to go check on the skull, but I decided I could be pretty sure it hadn't gone anywhere.

"Stupid," I muttered at my mirror as I braided my hair. I slapped on a little makeup and pulled on my oldest jeans and a sleeveless T-shirt. I might have to go by Mother's office, but I wasn't going to look like a junior executive. All her salespeople were sure I would go to work for Mother someday, completely disrupting their food chain. Actually, showing houses seemed like an attractive way to pass the time, and now that I had my own money—almost—I really might think about looking into it seriously.

But of course I didn't have to work for Mother. I gave the mirror a wicked grin, picturing the furor for a happy second, before I lapsed back to reality. Wrapping the band around the end of the braid to secure it, I admitted to myself that of course I would work for Mother if I did decide to take the plunge and switch jobs. But I'd miss the library, I told myself as I checked my purse to make sure I had everything. No I wouldn't, I realized suddenly. I'd miss the books. Not the job or the people.

The prospect of possibly resigning kept me entertained until I got to Great Day.

Amina's father was a bookkeeper, and of course he did the books for his wife's business. He was there when I came in, the bell over the door tinkling to announce my arrival. Miss Joe Nell was using some kind of hand-held steamer to get the wrinkles out of a newly arrived dress. She was a very attractive, fair woman in her middle forties. She'd been young when she had Amina, her only daughter. Amina's younger brother was still in graduate school. Miss Joe Nell was very religious, and, when my mother and father had gotten divorced when I was a teenager, one of my many fears was that Miss Joe Nell would disapprove of the divorce so much she wouldn't let me stay with Amina anymore. But Miss Joe Nell was a loving woman and sympathetic, too; my worry had been banished quickly.

Now she put down the steamer and gave me a hug.

"I just hope Amina's doing the right thing," she whispered.

"Well, I'm sure she is," I said with a confidence I was far from feeling. "I'm sure he's a good man."

"Oh, it's not him I worry about so much," Miss Joe Nell said, to my surprise. "It's Amina."

"We just hope she's really ready to settle this time," rumbled Mr. Day. He sang bass in the church choir, had for twenty years, and would until he could sing no more.

"I hope so, too," I admitted. And we all three looked at one another rather dolefully for a long second.

"Now, what kind of dress does Amina want me to try on?" I asked briskly.

Miss Joe Nell shook herself visibly and led me over to the formal dresses. "Let's see," she said. "Her dress, like I said, is mint green, with some white beading. I have it here, she tried on several things when she was home for your mother's wedding. I thought she was just sort of dreaming and planning, but I bet she had a little idea back then that they would move the date up."

The dress was beautiful. Amina would look like an American dream in it.

"So we can coordinate my dress easily," I said in an optimistic tone.

"Well, I looked at what we have in your size, and I found a few things that would look lovely with this shade of green. Even if you pick a solid in a different color, your bouquet could have green ribbons that would sort of tie it together..."

And we were off and running, deep in wedding talk.

I was glad I'd braided my hair that morning, because by the time I'd finished hauling dresses off and on it would have been a crow's nest otherwise. As it was, loose hairs crackling with electricity were floating around my face by the time I was done. One of the dresses became me and would coordinate, and, though I doubted I would ever have occasion to wear it again, I bought it. Mrs. Day tried to tell me she would pay for it, but I knew my bridesmaid's duty. Finally she let me have it at cost, and we both were satisfied. Amina's dress had long, see-through sleeves and solid cuffs, a simple neckline, beaded bodice, and a full skirt, plain enough to set off the bridal bouquet but fancy enough to be festive. My dress had short sleeves but the same neckline, and it was peach with a mint green cummerbund. I could get some heels dyed to match—in fact, I thought the heels I'd had dyed to match Linda Erhardt's bridesmaid's dress might do. I promised Miss Joe Nell I'd bring them by the store to check, since my dress had to remain at Great Day to have its hem raised.

And it had only taken an hour and a half, I discovered when I got back in my car. I remembered when I'd gone dress hunting with Sally Saxby and her mother, and four other bridesmaids. The expedition had consumed a whole very long day. It had taken me awhile to feel as fond of Sally as I had before we went dress hunting in Atlanta.

Of course, now Sally had been Mrs. Hunter for ten years and had a son almost as tall as me, and a daughter who took piano lessons.

No, I would *not* be depressed. The dress had been found, that was a good thing. I was going by the office, that was another good thing. Then I would go see the cats at the new house, as I was trying to think of it. Then I would treat myself to lunch somewhere good.

When I turned into the rear parking lot of my mother's office, I noticed no one dared to park in her space though she was actually out of the country. I pulled into it neatly, making a mental note to tell Mother this little fact. Mother, thinking "Teagarden Homes" was too long to fit on a Sold sign, had instead named her business Select Realty. Of course this was a blatant attempt to appeal to the "up" side of the market, and it seemed to have worked. Mother was a go-get'em realtor who never let business call her if she could get out there and beat the bushes for it first. She wanted every realtor she hired to be just as aggressive, and she didn't care what the applicant looked like as long as the right attitude came across. An injudicious rival had compared Select realtors to a school of sharks, in my hearing. Marching up the sidewalk to the old home Mother had bought and renovated beautifully, I found myself wondering if my mother would consider me a suitable employee.

Everyone who worked at Select Realty dressed to the nines, so I was fairly conspicuous, and I realized my choice of jeans and T-shirt had been a mistake. I had wanted to look as unlike a realtor as I could, and I had succeeded in looking like an outdated hippie.

Patty Cloud, at the front desk, was wearing a suit that cost as much as a week's salary from the library. And this was the *receptionist*.

"Aurora, how good to see you!" she said with a practiced smile. Patty was at least four years younger than me, but the suit and the artificial ease made her seem as much older.

Eileen Norris passed through the reception area to drop some papers labeled with a Post-it note on Patty's desk, and stopped in her tracks when she recognized me.

"My God, child, you look like something the cat dragged in!" Eileen bellowed. She was a suspiciously dark-haired woman about forty-five, with expensive clothes from the very best big women's store. Her makeup was heavy but well done, her perfume was intrusive but attractive, and she was one of the most overwhelming women I'd ever met. Eileen was something of a town character in Lawrenceton, and she could talk you into buying a house quicker than you could take an aspirin.

I wasn't exactly pleased with her greeting, but I'd made an error in judgment, and Eileen was not one to let that go by.

"I'm just dropping in to deliver a message. Mother is extending her honeymoon a little."

"I'm so glad she is," Eileen boomed. "That woman hadn't taken a vacation in a coon's age. I bet she's having a real good time."

"No doubt about it."

"And you're checking up on the children while their mama's away?"

There was also no doubt Eileen wasn't happy with the idea of the boss's daughter "checking up."

"Just wanted to see that the building was still standing," I said lightly. "But I do have a realty question to ask."

Mackie Knight, a young black realtor Mother had just taken on, came in just then with clients, a pair of newlyweds I recognized since their picture had been in the paper the same day Mother and John's had been. The couple looked a little dazed, and were arguing in a weary way between a house on Macree and a house on Littleton. Safely ahead of them, Mackie rolled his eyes at us as they passed through.

"He's working out good," Eileen said absently. "The younger couples don't mind having a black realtor, and the black clients love it. Now, you said you had a realty question?"

"Yes, I do. What are houses in the area right around the junior high selling for?"

Patty and Eileen snapped to attention. This was Business.

"How many bedrooms?"

"Ah—two."

"Square footage?"

"Maybe fourteen hundred."

"A house on Honor in that area just sold," Eileen said promptly. "Just a minute and I'll look that up."

She marched back to her desk, her high heels making little thumps on the carpet. I followed her through the unobtrusively attractive gray and blue halls to her office, second in size only to Mother's. It had probably been the second best bedroom. Mother had what had been the master bedroom, and the kitchen had the copying machine and a little snack area. The other rooms were much smaller and occupied by Mother's lesser minions. Eileen's desk was aggressively busy, papers everywhere, but they were in separate stacks, and she doubtless was capable of juggling many balls at a time.

"Honor, Honor," she muttered. She must have been looking up the price of the little house Arthur and Lynn had bought. Her ringed fingers flipped expertly through a stack of listings. "Here we go," she murmured. "Fifty-three," she said more loudly. "Are you interested in buying or selling?"

I could tell Eileen was no longer concerned with my blue jeans and messy braid.

"Maybe selling. I inherited the house right across the street from that house you're looking at now." I nodded at the listing sheet.

"Really," Eileen said, staring. "You? Inherited?"

"Yes."

"And you may want to sell the house instead of living in it?"

"Yes."

"Is the house paid for by the previous owner? The owner doesn't owe any money on it, I mean?"

"No, it's paid for." I thought I remembered Bubba Sewell telling me that. Yes, I did. Jane had been paying on the house until her mother died, when she'd had the cash to complete buying it in one whack.

"You have a completely free house and you don't want it? I would've thought a two bedroom was just the right size for you. Not that I wouldn't love to list it for you," Eileen said, recalled to her senses.

A frail, pretty woman in her late thirties stuck her head in. "Eileen, I'm off to show the Youngman house, if you've got the key handy," she said with a teasing smile.

"Idella! I can't believe I did it again!" Eileen hit her forehead with the heel of her hand, but very lightly so as not to smear her makeup.

"I'm sorry, I didn't know you had company," the woman continued.

"Idella, this is Aurora Teagarden, Aida's daughter," Eileen said, rummaging through her purse. "Aurora, you may not know Idella Yates yet? She came in with us earlier this year."

While Idella and I exchanged nice-to-meet-you's, Eileen kept up with her search. Finally she unearthed a key with a large label attached. "Idella, I'm sorry," Eileen boomed. "I don't know why I don't remember to put the keys back on the keyboard. That seems to be one thing I cannot remember. We're supposed to put them back on the main keyboard, that Patty watches, every time we use a key to show a house," Eileen explained to me. "But for some reason, I just cannot get it through my head."

"Don't worry about it," Idella said sweetly, and with a nod to me she left to go show the house. She did glance at her watch rather pointedly as she left, letting Eileen know that, if she was late to meet her client, Eileen was the one to blame.

Eileen sat staring after Idella with a curiously uneasy look on her face. Eileen's face was only used to positive emotions, emerging full-blown. Something like "uneasy" sat very oddly on her strong features.

"There's something funny about that woman," Eileen said abruptly and dismissively. Her face fell back into more familiar lines. "Now, about that house—do you know things like how old the roof is, whether it's on city water, how old the house itself is? Though I think all the houses in that area were built about nineteen fifty-five or so. Maybe some in the early sixties."

"If I make up my mind definitely, I'll get all that information," I promised, wondering how on earth I'd find out about the roof. I might have to go through every one of Jane's receipts, unless perhaps one of her neighbors might remember the roofing crew. Roofing crews usually made their presence felt. A vagrant thought crossed my mind. What if one of the houses was older than it appeared, or had been built on the site of a much older home? Maybe there was a basement or a tunnel under one of the houses where the body had been until it had been tossed into the weeds at the end of the street?

Admittedly this was a pretty stupid idea, and when I asked Eileen about it she dismissed it as it deserved. "Oh, no," she said briskly, beginning to shake her head before I even finished my sentence. "What a strange notion, Roe. That area is much too low for basements, and there wasn't anything there before the junior high was built. It was timberland."

Eileen insisted on walking me out of the office. I decided it was because I was a potential client, rather than because I was Aurora Teagarden. Eileen was not a toady.

"Now, when is your mother coming back?" she asked.

"Oh, soon, sometime this week. She wasn't definite. She just didn't want to call in to the office; maybe she was scared if she talked to one of you she'd just get to talking about work. She was just using me as a messenger to you all." All of the other offices that I passed were busy or showed signs of work in progress. Phones were ringing, papers were being copied, briefcases were being packed with paperwork.

For the first time in my life, I wondered how much money my mother had. Now that I didn't need it anymore, I was finally curious. Money was something we never talked about. She had enough for her, and did her kind of thing—expensive clothes, a very luxurious car (she said it impressed clients), and some good jewelry. She didn't play any sport; for exercise she had installed a treadmill in one of the bedrooms of her house. But she sold a lot of real estate, and I assumed she got a percentage from the sales of the realtors she employed. I was very fuzzy on how that worked, because I'd just never thought it was my business. In a moment I was not too proud of, I wondered if she'd made a new will now that John and she had married. I frowned at myself in the rearview mirror as I sat at a stoplight.

Of course, John already had plenty of money of his own, and he had two sons . . .

I shook my head impatiently, trying to shake those bad thoughts loose. I tried to excuse myself by reasoning that it was really no wonder that I was will- and death-conscious lately, or for that matter that I was more than usually interested in money matters. But I wasn't happy with myself, so I was quicker to be displeased when I pulled into the driveway of the house on Honor to find Bubba Sewell waiting for me.

It was as if I'd conjured him up by thinking about him.

"Hello," I said cautiously as I got out of the car. He got out of his and strode over to me.

"I took a chance on finding you here. I called the library and found out you were off today."

"Yes, I don't work every day," I said unnecessarily. "I came to check on the kittens."

"Kittens." His heavy eyebrows flew up behind his glasses.

"Madeleine came back. She had kittens in the closet in Jane's room."

"Have Parnell and Leah been over here?" he asked. "Have they given you much trouble?"

"I think Parnell feels we're even now that I have four kittens to find homes for," I said.

Bubba laughed, but he didn't sound like he meant it.

"Listen," he began, "the county bar association dinner-dance is next weekend and I wondered if you would go with me?"

I was so surprised I almost gaped at him. Not only was he reportedly dating my beautiful friend Lizanne, but also I could have sworn that Bubba Sewell was not the least bit interested in me as a woman. And though my dating schedule was certainly not heavy, I had learned long ago that it was better to be home alone with a good book and a bag of potato chips than it was to be out on a date with someone who left you cold.

"I'm sorry, Bubba," I said. I was not accustomed enough to turning down dates to be good at it. "I'm just very busy right now. But thank you for asking me."

He looked away, embarrassed. "Okay. Maybe some other time."

I smiled as noncommittally as I could.

"Is everything going—all right?" he asked suddenly.

How much did he know?

"You read about the bones found around the dead end sign?" It had been below the report about Bubba's run for representative: CITY WORKERS FIND BONES. It had been a very short story; I expected a much fuller account in the next morning's paper.

Maybe, I suddenly thought, now that the law had the bones, there would be more information on the sex and age of the skeleton included in the next story. The few paragraphs this morning had stated that the bones were going to a pathologist for examination. I swam out of my thoughts to find Bubba Sewell eyeing me with some apprehension.

"The bones?" he prompted. "A skeleton?"

"Well, there wasn't a skull," I murmured.

"Was that in the paper?" he asked sharply. I'd made a mistake; as a matter of fact, the skeleton's skull-lessness had not been mentioned in the story.

"Gosh, Bubba," I said coolly. "I just don't know."

We stared at each other for a minute.

"Gotta be going," I said finally. "The cats are waiting."

"Oh, sure." He tucked his mouth in and then relaxed it. "Well...if you really need me, you know where I am. By the way, had you heard I'm running for office?"

"Yes. I'd heard that, sure had." And we looked at each other for a second more. Then I marched up the sidewalk and unlocked the front door. Madeleine slithered out instantly and headed for the soft dirt around the bushes. Her litter box was only a backup system: she preferred to go out-of-doors. Bubba Sewell was gone by the time I locked the front door behind me.

TEN

I RATTLED AROUND restlessly in the "new" house for a few hours. It was mine, all mine, but somehow I didn't feel too cheerful about that anymore. Actually, I preferred my town house, a soulless rental. It had more room, I was used to it, I like having an upstairs I didn't have to clean if company was coming. Could I stand living across the street from Arthur and Lynn? Next door to the unpredictable Marcia Rideout? Jane's books were already cramming the bookcases. Where would I put mine? But if I sold this house and bought a bigger one, probably the yard would be bigger, and I haven't ever taken care of one... If Torrance hadn't mowed the yard for me, I wouldn't know how to cope. Maybe the yard crew that did the lawn at the town houses?

I maundered on in my head, opening the kitchen cabinets and shutting them, trying to decide which pots and pans were duplicates of mine so I could take them to the local Baptist church, which kept a room of household goods for families who got burned out or suffered some equal disaster. I finally chose some in a lackadaisical way and carried them out to the car loose; I was out of boxes. I was treading water emotionally, unable to settle on any one task or course of action.

I wanted to quit my job.

I was scared to. Jane's money seemed too good to be true. Somehow, I feared it might be taken away from me.

I wanted to throw the skull in the lake. I was also scared of whoever had reduced the skull to its present state.

I wanted to sell Jane's house because I didn't particularly care for it. I wanted to live in it because it was safely mine.

I wanted Aubrey Scott to adore me; surely a minister would have a specially beautiful wedding? I did not want to marry Aubrey Scott because being a minister's wife took a lot more internal fortitude than I had. A proper minister's wife would have marched out of the house with that skull and gone straight to the police station without a second thought. But Aubrey seemed too serious a man to date without the prospect of the relationship evolving in that direction.

I did run the pots and pans to the Baptist church, where I was thanked so earnestly that it was soothing, and made me think better of my poor character.

On the way back to the new house, I stopped at Jane's bank on impulse. I had the key with me, surely? Yes, here it was in my purse. I went in hesitantly, suddenly thinking that the bank might present difficulties about letting me see the safe deposit box. But it wasn't too difficult. I had to explain to three people, but then one of them remembered Bubba Sewell coming by, and that made everything all right. Accompanied by a woman in a sober business suit, I got Jane's safe deposit box. Something about those vaults where they're kept makes me feel that there's going to be a dreadful secret inside. All those locked boxes, the heavy door, the attendant! I went into the little room that held only a table and a single chair, shut the door. Then I opened the box, telling myself firmly that nothing dreadful could be in a box so small. Nothing dreadful, but a good deal that was beautiful. When I saw the contents of the long metal box, I let my breath out in a single sigh. Who would ever have imagined that Jane would want these things?

There was a pin shaped like a bow, made out of garnets with the center knot done in diamonds. There were garnet and diamond earrings to match. There was a slim gold chain with a single emerald on it, and a pearl necklace and bracelet. There were a few rings, none of them spectacular or probably extremely valuable, but all of them expensive and very pretty. I felt I had opened the treasure chest in the pirate's cave. And these were mine now! I could not attach any sentiment to them, because I'd never seen Jane wear them—perhaps the pearls, yes; she'd worn the pearls to a wedding we'd both attended. Nothing else rang any bells. I tried on the rings. They were only a little loose. Jane and I both had small fingers. I was trying to imagine what I could wear the bow pin and earrings to; they'd look great on a winter white suit, I decided. But as I held the pieces and touched them, I knew that despite Bubba Sewell's saying there was nothing else in the safe deposit box, I was disappointed that there was no letter from Jane.

After I'd driven back to the house, despite an hour spent watching Madeleine and her kittens, I still could not ground myself. I ended up throwing myself on the couch and turning on CNN, while reading some of my favorite passages from Jane's copy of Donald Rumbelow's book on Jack the Ripper. She had marked her place with a slip of paper, and for a moment my heart pounded, thinking Jane had left me another message, something more explicit than *I didn't do it*. But it was only an old grocery list: eggs, nutmeg, tomatoes, butter...

I sat up on the couch. Just because this piece of paper had been a false alarm didn't mean there weren't any other notes! Jane would put them where she would think I'd find them. She had known no one but me would go through her books.

The first one had been in a book about Madeleine Smith, Jane's main field of study. I riffled through Jane's other books about the Smith case. I shook them.

Nothing.

Then maybe she'd hidden something in one of the books about the case that most intrigued me— well, which one would that be? Either Jack the Ripper or the murder of Julia Wallace. I was already reading Jane's only Ripper book. I flipped through it but found no other notes. Jane also had only one book on Julia Wallace, and there again I found no message. Theodore Durrant, Thompson-Bywater, Sam Sheppard, Reginald Christie, Crippen...I shook Jane's entire true-crime library with no results.

I went through her fictional crime, heavy on women writers; Margery Allingham, Mary Roberts Rinehart, Agatha Christie...the older school of mysteries. And Jane had an unexpected shelf of sword-and-sorcery science fiction, too. I didn't bother with those, at least initially; Jane would not have expected me to look there.

But in the end I went through those as well. After two hours, I had shaken, riffled, and otherwise disturbed every volume on the shelves, only a trace of common sense preventing me from flinging them on the floor as I finished. I'd even read all the envelopes in the letter rack on the kitchen wall, the kind you buy at a handcraft fair; all the letters seemed to be from charities or old friends, and I stuffed them irritably back in the rack to go through at a later date.

Jane had left me no other messages. I had the money, the house, the cat (plus kittens), the skull, and the note that said *I didn't do it*.

A peremptory knock on the front door made me jump. I'd been sitting on the floor so lost in the doldrums I hadn't heard anyone approach. I scrambled up and looked through the peephole, then flung the door open. The woman outside was as well-groomed as Marcia Rideout, as cool as a cucumber; she was not sweating in the heat. She was five inches taller than me. She looked like Lauren Bacall.

"Mother!" I said happily, and gave her a brief hug. She undoubtedly loved me, but she didn't like her clothes wrinkled.

"Aurora," she murmured, and gave my hair a stroke.

"When did you get back? Come in!"

"I got in really late last night," she explained, coming into the room and staring around her. "I tried to call you this morning after we got up, but you weren't home. You weren't at the library. So after a while, I decided I'd phone in to the office, and Eileen told me about the house. Who is this woman who left you the house?"

"How's John?"

"No, don't put me off. You know I'll tell you all about the trip later."

"Jane Engle. John knows—John knew her, too. She was in Real Murders with us."

"At least that's disbanded now," Mother said with some relief. It would have been hard for Mother to send John off to a monthly meeting of a club she considered only just on the good side of obscenity.

"Yes. Well, Jane and I were friends through the club, and she never married, so when she died, she left me—her estate."

"Her estate," my mother repeated. Her voice was beginning to get a decided edge. "And just what, if you don't mind my asking, does that estate consist of?"

I could tell her or I could stonewall her. If I didn't tell her, she'd just pull strings until she found out, and she had a bunch of strings to pull.

"This Jane Engle was the daughter of Mrs. John Elgar Engle," I said.

"The Mrs. Engle who lived in that gorgeous mansion on Ridgemont? The one that sold for eight hundred and fifty thousand because it needed renovation?"

Trust Mother to know her real estate.

"Yes, Jane was the daughter of that Mrs. Engle."

"There was a son, wasn't there?"

"Yes, but he died."

"That was only ten or fifteen years ago. She couldn't have spent all that money, living here." Mother had sized up the house instantly.

"I think this house was almost paid for when old Mrs. Engle died," I said.

"So you got this house," Mother said, "and . . . ?"

"And five hundred and fifty thousand dollars," I said baldly. "Thereabouts. And some jewelry."

Mother's mouth dropped open. It was the first time in my life I think I'd ever astonished my mother. She's not a money-grubbing person, but she has a great respect for cash and property, and it is the way she measures her own success as a professional. She sat down rather abruptly on the couch and automatically crossed her elegant legs in their designer sportswear. She will go so far as to wear slacks on vacation, to pool parties, and on days she doesn't work; she would rather be mugged than wear shorts.

"And of course I now have the cat and her kittens," I continued maliciously.

"The cat," Mother repeated in a dazed way.

Just then the feline in question made her appearance, followed by a chorus of forlorn mews from the kittens in Jane's closet. Mother uncrossed her legs and leaned forward to look at

Madeleine as if she had never seen a cat before. Madeleine walked right up to Mother's feet, stared up at her for a moment, then leaped onto the couch in one flowing motion and curled up on Mother's lap. Mother was so horrified she didn't move.

"This," she said, "is a cat you inherited?"

I explained about Parnell Engle, and Madeleine's odyssey to have her kittens in "her" house.

Mother neither touched Madeleine nor heaved her legs to remove her.

"What breed is she?" Mother asked stiffly.

"She's a mutt cat," I said, surprised. Then I realized Mother was evaluating the cat. Or valuing her. "Want me to move her?"

"Please," my mother said, still in that stiff voice.

Finally I understood. My mother was scared of the cat. In fact, she was terrified. But, being Mother, she would never admit it. That was why we'd never had cats when I was growing up. All her arguments about animal hair on everything, having to empty a litter tray, were just so much smoke screen.

"Are you scared of dogs, too?" I asked, fascinated. I carefully scooped Madeleine off Mother's lap, and scratched her behind the ears as I held her. She obviously preferred Mother's lap, but put up with me a few seconds, then indicated she wanted down. She padded into the kitchen to use her litter box, followed by Mother's horrified gaze. I pushed my glasses up on my nose so I could have a clear view of this unprecedented sight.

"Yes," Mother admitted. Then she took her eyes off Madeleine and saw my face. Her guard snapped up immediately. "I've just never cared for pets. For God's sake, go get yourself some contact lenses so you'll stop fiddling with those glasses," she said very firmly. "So. Now you have a lot of money?"

"Yes," I admitted, still enthralled by my new knowledge of my mother.

"What are you going to do?"

"I don't know. I haven't made any plans yet. Of course, the estate has to go through probate, but that shouldn't take too long, Bubba Sewell says."

"He's the lawyer who's handling the estate?"

"Yes, he's the executor."

"He's sharp."

"Yes, I know."

"He's ambitious."

"He's running for office."

"Then he'll do everything right. Running for office has become just like running under a microscope."

"He asked me out, but I turned him down."

"Good idea," my mother said, to my surprise. "It's never wise to have a social relationship mixed up with money transactions or financial arrangements."

I wondered what she would say about a social relationship mixed up with religion.

"So you had a good time?" I asked.

"Yes, we did. But John came down with something like the flu, so we had to come home. He's over the worst, and I expect he'll be out and about tomorrow."

"He didn't want to stay there until he got over it?" I couldn't imagine traveling with the flu.

"I suggested it, but he said when he was sick, he didn't want to be in a resort where everyone else was having fun, he wanted to be home in his own bed. He was quite stubborn about it. But, up until that time, we really had a great honeymoon." Mother's face looked almost soft as she said that, and it was borne in on me for the first time that my mother was in love, maybe not in as gooey a way as Amina, but she was definitely feeling the big rush.

It occurred to me that John had come back to Lawrenceton and gotten in Mother's bed, not his own. "Has John sold his house yet?" I asked.

"One of his sons wanted it," Mother said in as noncommittal a voice as she could manage. "Avery, the one that's expecting the baby. It's a big old house, as you know."

"How did John David feel about that? Not that it's any of my business." John David was John's second son.

"I wouldn't have presumed to advise John about his family business," Mother began answering indirectly, "because John and I signed a prenuptial agreement about our financial affairs."

This was news to me, and I felt a distinct wave of relief. I'd never considered it before, but all the complications that could arise when both parties had grown children suddenly occurred to me. I'd only thought of what Mother might leave when she died, this very day. I should have known, as property conscious as she was, she would have taken care of everything.

"So I didn't advise him," Mother was continuing, "but he thought out loud when he was trying to figure out what was fair to do."

"You're the obvious person for input when it comes to real estate questions."

"Well, he did ask me the value of the house on the current market."

"And?"

"I had it appraised, and I think—now I don't know, but I think—he gave John David the cash value of the house, and deeded over the house to Avery."

"So John David didn't want the house at all?"

"No, his work requires that he transfer every few years, and it didn't make sense for him to own a house in Lawrenceton."

"That worked out well."

"Now I'm going to tell you what I did about my house."

"Oh, Mom!" I protested.

"No," she said firmly. "You need to know this."

"Okay," I said reluctantly.

"I think a man needs to know he has a home that's his," she said. "And since John gave up his house, I have left him mine for his lifetime. So if I die before John, he gets to stay in the house until he dies. I thought that was only right. But, after John passes away, it's yours to do with as you will, of course."

This was just my season for having things willed to me. Suddenly I realized that Mother would leave me her business and her money, as well as the house; with Jane's money, and her little house, too, I need never work another day in my life.

What a startling prospect.

"Whatever you do is fine with me," I said hastily, aware that Mother was looking at me in a funny way. "I don't want to talk about it."

"We'll have to sometime," Mother warned.

What was with her today? Had getting remarried somehow awakened or reinforced her feelings of her own mortality? Was it signing the prenuptial agreement with all these arrangements for what would happen after her death? She was just back from her honeymoon. She should be feeling pretty frisky.

"Why are you talking about all this now?" I asked bluntly.

She considered this. "I don't know," she said in a puzzled way. "I certainly didn't come here expecting to talk about it. I was going to tell you about the hotel and the beach and the tour we took, but somehow I got sidetracked. Maybe when we talked about what Jane Engle left you, I started thinking about what I was going to leave you. Though, of course, now you won't need it as badly. It does seem strange to me that Jane left all her money and property to someone who isn't even a member of the family, someone who wasn't even that close a friend."

"It seems strange to me, too, Mom," I admitted. I didn't want to tell my mother that Jane had left everything to me because she saw me starting out like her, single and bookish, and maybe Jane had seen something else in me that struck a chord with her; we were both fascinated by death between the pages of a book. "And it's going to seem strange to a lot of other people."

She thought about that for a little. She waited delicately to see if I would enlighten her about Jane's motives.

"I'm glad for you," Mother said after a minute, seeing I wasn't going to offer any more information about my relationship with Jane. "And I don't expect we have to worry about what people say."

"Thanks."

"I'd better get back to my sick husband," Mother said fondly.

How strange it was to hear that. I smiled at her without thinking about it. "I'm glad for you, too," I told her honestly.

"I know that." She gathered her purse and keys, and I rose to walk her to her car.

She was discussing a dinner party an old friend was planning to give for her and John, and I was wondering if I should ask to bring Aubrey, when Marcia Rideout came out of her front door. She was wearing another matched and beautifully ironed shorts set, and her hair was a little blonder, it seemed to me.

"Is that your momma I see with you?" she called when she was halfway down her drive. "Do you just have a minute?"

We both waited with polite, expectant smiles.

"Aida, you may not remember me," Marcia said, with her head tilted coyly to one side, "but you and I were on the Fallfest committee together a couple of years ago."

"Oh, of course," Mother said, professional warmth in her voice. "The festival turned out very well that year, didn't it?"

"Yes, but it was sure a lot of work, more than I ever bargained for! Listen, we're all just so thrilled Roe is moving on our street. I don't know if she told you yet or not, I understand you've been away on your honeymoon, but Torrance and I are giving Aurora and our other new neighbors"—and Marcia nodded her smooth head at the little yellow-shuttered house across the street—"a little get-together tomorrow night. We would just love it if you and your new husband could come."

Nothing nonpluses Mother. "We'd love to, but I'm afraid John came back from the Bahamas with just a touch of flu," she explained. "I tell you what, I may just drop in by myself for a few minutes, just to meet Aurora's new neighbors. If my husband is feeling better, maybe he'll come, too. Can I leave it that indefinite?"

"Oh, of course, that poor man, the flu in this pretty weather! And on his honeymoon! Bless his heart!"

"Who are the other new people on the street?" Mother inquired, to stem Marcia's pity.

"A police detective and his brand-new wife, who is also a police detective! And she's going to have a baby just any time now. Isn't that exciting? I don't think I'd ever met a real detective until they moved in, and now we have two of them on the street. We should all be real safe now! We've had a lot of break-ins on this street the past few years—but I'm sure your daughter is as safe as can be, now," Marcia tacked on hastily.

"Would that detective be Arthur Smith?" Mother asked. I heard the permafrost under her words. I could feel my face begin to tighten. I had never known how much Mother knew or guessed about my relationship with Arthur, but I had a feeling she'd gotten a pretty accurate picture. I turned my face away a little under pretext of pushing up my glasses.

"Yes. He's such a solemn young man, and handsome, too. Of course, not as handsome as the man Roe is dating." Marcia actually winked.

"You don't think so?" my mother said agreeably. I bit my upper lip.

"Oh, no. That minister is so tall and dark. You can tell from my marrying Torrance, I like tall, dark men. And that mustache! It may not be nice to say this about a man in the ministry, but it's just plain sexy."

My mother had been totting up this description. "Well, I'll sure try to come, thanks so much for inviting me," she said in a perfectly polite but unmistakably conclusive way.

"I'll just go back to cleaning the house," Marcia said brightly, and, after a chorus of good-byes, off she trotted.

"Dating Father Scott?" Mother asked when she was sure Marcia was out of earshot. "And you're over that lousy policeman?"

"Yes to both."

Mother looked quite unsettled for a minute. "You turned down a date with Bubba Sewell, you're over that Arthur Smith, and you're dating a minister," she said wonderingly. "There's hope for your love life after all."

As I waved to her as she drove down the street, it was a positive satisfaction for me to think of the skull in her blanket bag.

ELEVEN

IN A BURST OF morning energy, I was singing in the shower when the telephone rang. Blessing answering machines, I barely paused in my rendition of "The Star-Spangled Banner." The shower is probably the only place our national anthem should be sung, especially by people with a limited vocal range, a category that definitely includes me. As I rinsed the shampoo out of my hair, I did a medley of my favorite ads. For my finale, as I toweled I warbled "Three Little Ducks."

There is something to be said for living by oneself when one wants to sing unheard.

It would be hard to say why I was in such a festive mood. I had to go in to work for five hours, then come back to the town house to prepare for the party. I was pleased at the prospect of seeing Aubrey, but not goo-goo eyed. I was more or less getting used to being rich by now (though the word still gave me a thrill up my spine), and I was on standby regarding action on the skull. I squinted into my makeup mirror as I put on a little eye shadow.

"I'm going to quit my job," I told my reflection, smiling.

The *pleasure* of being able to say that! To decide, just like that! Money was wonderful.

I remembered the phone message and pressed the play button, beaming at my reflection in the mirror like an idiot, my drying hair beginning to fly around my head in a dark, wavy nimbus.

"Roe?" began the voice, faint and uncertain. "This is Robin Crusoe, calling from Italy. I called in and got your message from Phil . . . the guy subletting my apartment. Are you all right? He said Arthur married someone else. Can I come see you when I get back from Europe? If that's not a good idea, send a note to my old address. Well, write me either way, and I'll get it when I get back. That should be in a few weeks, probably late next month. Or earlier, I'm running out of money. Good-bye."

I had frozen when I first heard the voice begin. Now I sat breathing shallowly for a few seconds, my brush in my hand, my teeth biting my lower lip gently. My heart was beating fast, I'll admit. Robin had been my tenant and my friend and almost my lover. I really wanted to see him again. Now I would have the pleasure of composing a note that would say very delicately that I *definitely* wanted him to come calling when he got back. I didn't want him to get the impression I was sitting in Lawrenceton with my tongue hanging out while I panted, but I did want him to come, if he was of the same mind in a few weeks. And if I was. I could take my time composing that note.

I brushed my hair, which began to crackle and fly around even more wildly. I gathered it all together and put a band on it about halfway down its length, not as stodgy as a "real" ponytail. And I tied a frivolous bow around the band. However, I did wear one of my old "librarian" outfits that so disgusted Amina: a solid navy skirt of neutral length with a navy-and-white-striped blouse, plain support hose, and unattractive but very comfortable shoes. I cleaned my glasses, pushed them up on my nose, nodded at my reflection in the full-length mirror, and went downstairs.

If I'd known how to cha-cha, I think I would have done it going up the ramp from the employees' parking lot into the library.

"Aren't we happy today?" Lillian said sourly, sipping from her cup of coffee at the worktable in the book-mending room.

"Yes, ma'am, we are," I said, depositing my purse in my little locker and snapping the padlock shut. My only claim to fame in my history as a librarian in Lawrenceton was that I had never once lost my padlock key. I kept it on a safety pin and pinned it to my skirt or my slip or my blouse. Today I pinned it to my collar and marched off to Mr. Clerrick's office, humming a military tune. Or what I imagined was a military tune.

I tapped on the half-open door and stuck my head in. Mr. Clerrick was already at work on a heap of papers, a steaming cup of coffee at his elbow and a cigarette in the ashtray smoldering.

"Good morning, Roe," he said, looking up from his desk. Sam Clerrick was married with four daughters, and, since he worked in a library, that meant he was surrounded by women from the moment he got up to the moment he went to bed. You would think he would have learned how to treat them. But his greatest and most conspicuous failure was in people management. No one would ever accuse Sam Clerrick of coddling anyone, or of favoritism; he didn't care for any of us, had no idea what our home lives were like, and made no allowances for any individual's personality or work preferences. No one would ever like him; he would never be accused of being unfair.

I had always been a little nervous around someone who played his emotional cards as close to his chest as Sam Clerrick. Suddenly leaving did not seem so simple.

"I'm going to quit my job," I said quietly, while I still had some nerve. As he stared, that little bit of nerve began to trickle away. "I'm on part-time anyway, I don't feel like you really need me anymore."

He kept peering at me over his half-glasses. "Are you giving me notice, or quitting, no more work as of today?" he asked finally.

"I don't know," I said foolishly. After I considered a moment, I said, "Since you have at least three substitute librarians on your call list, and I know at least two of them would love to go regular part-time, I'm quitting, no more work as of five hours from now."

"Is there something wrong that we can talk about?"

I came all the way into the room. "Working here is okay," I told him. "I just don't have to anymore, financially, and I feel like a change."

"You don't need the money," he said in amazement.

He was probably the only person working at the library, or perhaps the only person in Lawrenceton, who didn't know by now about the money.

"I inherited."

"My goodness, your mother didn't die, I hope?" He actually put his pencil down, so great was his concern.

"No, no relative."

"Oh—good. Well. I'm sorry to see you go, even though you were certainly our most notorious employee for a while last year. Well, it's been longer than that now, I suppose."

"Did you think about firing me then?"

"Actually, I was holding off until you killed Lillian."

I stared at him blankly until I accepted the amazing fact that Sam Clerrick had made a joke. I began laughing, and he began laughing, and suddenly he looked like a human being.

"It's been a pleasure," I said, meaning it for the first time, and turned and left his office.

"Your insurance will last for thirty days," he called after me, running a little truer to form.

As luck would have it, that morning at the library business was excruciatingly slow. I didn't want to tell anyone I'd quit until I was actually leaving, so I hid among the books all morning, reading the shelves, dusting, and piddling along. I didn't get a lunch break, since I was just working five hours; I was supposed to bring it with me or get one of the librarians going out to bring back something from a fast-food place, and eat it very quickly. But that would mean eating in the break room, and there was sure to be someone else in there, and having a conversation without revealing my intention would be seen as fraudulent, in a way. So I dodged from here to there, making myself scarce, and by two o'clock I was very hungry. Then I had to go through the ritual of saying good-bye, I enjoyed working with you, I'll be in often to get books so we'll be seeing each other.

It made me sadder than I thought it would. Even saying good-bye to Lillian was not the unmitigated pleasure I had expected. I would miss having her around because she made me feel so virtuous and smart by contrast, I realized with shame. (*I* didn't moan and groan about every little change in work routine, *I* didn't bore people to tears with detailed accounts of boring events, *I* knew who Benvenuto Cellini was.) And I remembered Lillian finally standing by me when things had been so bad during the murders months before.

"Maybe you can hunt for a husband full-time now," Lillian said in parting, and my shame vanished completely. Then I read in Lillian's face the knowledge that the only thing she had that I could possibly want was a husband.

"We'll see," I told her, and held my hands behind my back so I wouldn't choke her.

I retrieved my purse and turned in my locker key, and I walked out the back door for the last time.

I went straight to the grocery store. I wanted something for lunch, I wanted something to put in the refrigerator at the house on Honor for snacks while I was there. I zoomed through the grocery store tossing boxes and produce bags in my cart with abandon. I celebrated quitting my job by getting one of the really expensive microwave meals, the kind with a neat reusable plate. This was getting fancy for me, for lunch anyway. Maybe now I would have time to cook. Did I want to learn to cook in any more detail? I could make spaghetti, and I could make pecan pie. Did I need to know anything else? I debated it as I stood in front of the microwave at the town house.

I could decide at my leisure. I was now a woman of leisure.

I liked the sound of it.

The woman of leisure decided to celebrate by buying a new outfit to wear to the Rideouts' party. I would not go to Great Day, I decided; I'd share the wealth and go to Marcus Hatfield instead. Usually Marcus Hatfield made me nervous; though it was a mere satellite of the big Atlanta store, the selection was just too great, the saleswomen too aggressively groomed. Maybe my contact with Marcia was inuring me to immaculate grooming; I felt I could face even the cosmetics-counter woman without flinching.

I pulled my skirt straight and stiffened my spine before I entered. I can buy anything in this store, I reminded myself. I marched through the doors in my hopeless librarian's outfit. I was almost immediately confronted by a curvy vision in bright flowers, perfect nails, and subtle makeup.

"Hey, neighbor," exclaimed the vision. It was Carey Osland in her working getup. I could see why she preferred loafers and housedresses. She looked marvelous, almost edible, but definitely not comfortable. "I'm glad to see you," Carey was saying warmly while I was decoding her identity.

"Good to see you, too," I managed.

"Can I help you today?"

"I need something new to wear tonight."

"To the sun-deck party."

"Yes. It's so nice of the Rideouts to be giving it."

"Marcia loves to entertain. There's nothing she likes better than to have a bunch of people over."

"She said she didn't like it when her husband had to be away overnight."

"No. I expect you noticed she drinks a little then. She's been like that as long as I've known her, I guess... though I don't know her very well. She knows a lot of people around town, but she never seems to be close friends with anyone. Were you thinking of a sports outfit or did you want a sundress, something like that?"

"What?"

"For the party."

"Oh, sorry, I was off in the clouds somewhere. Um... what are you going to wear?"

"Oh, I'm too fat to wear a sundress," Carey said cheerfully. "But you'd look real pretty in one; and, so it wouldn't be too dressy, you could wear flat sandals and go real plain on your jewelry."

I looked dubiously at the dress Carey had pulled out. Mrs. Day would never have suggested it for me. But, then, Mrs. Day didn't carry too much like this at her shop. It was orange-and-white, very pretty but very casual, and there wasn't a back to it.

"I couldn't wear a bra with that," I pointed out.

"Oh, no," Carey agreed calmly.

"I would jiggle," I said doubtfully.

"Go try it on," Carey said with a wink. "If you don't like it, we have all kinds of cute shorts sets and lightweight pants, and any of them would be just fine, but just put this dress on."

I had never had to almost completely undress to try on clothes before. I pulled on the dress and bounced up and down on the balls of my feet, my eyes on the dressing-room mirror. I was trying to gauge the amount of jiggle. I am chesty for such a small person, and there was enough jiggle to give me pause.

"How is it?" Carey called from outside my cubicle.

"Oh...I don't know," I said doubtfully. I bounced again. "After all, I'm going with a minister."

"He's human," Carey observed. "God made bosoms, too."

"True." I turned around and observed my back. It looked very bare. "I can't carry this off, Carey," I told her.

"Let me see."

I reluctantly opened the door of the cubicle.

"Wow," said Carey. "You really look *good*," she said with squinted eyes. "Very sexy," she added in a conspiratorial whisper.

"I just feel too conspicuous. My back feels cold."

"He'd love it."

"I don't know about that."

I looked in a bigger mirror at the end of the row of dressing rooms. I considered. No, I decided finally. I could not go out in that dress with someone I hadn't slept with.

"I'm not going to wear it tonight, so I still need to find something else for that," I told Carey. "But I think I'll buy it anyway."

Carey became the complete saleswoman. The orange-and-white dress was whisked away to be put on a hanger, and she brought several more things for me to try on. Carey seemed to be determined that I wanted to present a sexy, sophisticated image, and I became sorry I hadn't gone to Great Day. Finally we found a cotton knit shorts and shirt that represented a compromise. The shirt was scoop-necked and white with red polka dots, and the red shorts were cut very full, like a little skirt, with a long tie belt that matched the shirt. I certainly had a lot of exposed skin, but at least it wasn't on my back. Carey talked me into red sandals and red bracelet and earrings to match before I called a halt to my shopping.

When I carried my purchases back to the town house, I called Aubrey at his church. "Who's calling?" the church secretary asked, when I wanted to be connected to Aubrey.

"Roe Teagarden."

"Oh!" she said breathlessly. "Sure, Roe, I'll tell him. He's such a nice man, we just love him here at St. John."

I stared at the phone for a second before I realized I was being given a boost in my assumed effort to win the heart of their priest. The congregation of St. John's must think it was time their leader married again, and I must be respectable enough at first glance to qualify as a suitable mate.

"Roe?"

"Hi, Aubrey," I said, shaking myself out of my thoughts. "Listen, would you meet me tonight at the house on Honor instead of picking me up here at the town house? I want to feed the cat before the party."

"Sure. Are we supposed to bring anything? A bottle of wine?"

"She didn't want me to bring anything to eat, but if you want to bring a bottle of wine, I imagine they'd be glad." A nice thought on Aubrey's part.

"This is casual, right?"

"It's going to be on their sun deck, so I'm sure it is."

"Good. I'll see you at your new house at seven, then."

"That's just fine."

"I look forward to it," he said quietly.

"Me, too."

I GOT THERE EARLY, and pulled my car all the way inside the carport so there'd be room for Aubrey's. After tending to Madeleine's needs, I thought of the clothes still in Jane's drawers. I'd cleaned out the closet, but not the chest of drawers. I pulled one open idly to see what I had to contend with. It turned out to be Jane's sleepwear drawer. Jane had had an unexpected taste in nightgowns. These certainly weren't what I'd call little-old-lady gowns, though they weren't naughty or anything like that. I pulled out the prettiest, a rose pink nylon, and decided I might actually keep it. Then I thought, Maybe I'll just spend the night here. Somehow the idea struck me as fun. The sheets on the bed were clean, changed by the maid hired to straighten everything out after Jane had gone into the hospital. Here was a gown. I'd just put a little food in the refrigerator. The air conditioner was running. There was a toothbrush in a sealed container in the bathroom, and an unopened tube of toothpaste. I would see what waking up in my new house was like.

The doorbell rang, announcing Aubrey's arrival. I answered it feeling a little self-conscious because of the scoop neckline. Sure enough, Aubrey's eyes went instantly to my cleavage. "You should have seen the one I didn't wear," I said defensively.

"Was I that obvious?" he said, a little embarrassed.

"Carey Osland says God made bosoms, too," I told him, and then closed my eyes and wished the ground would swallow me up.

"Carey Osland says truly," he said fervently. "You look great."

Aubrey had a knack for taking the embarrassment out of situations.

"You look nice yourself," I told him. He was wearing what would be a safe outfit at ninety percent of Lawrenceton's social occasions; a navy knit shirt and khaki slacks, with loafers.

"Well, now that we've admired each other, isn't it time to go?"

I glanced at my watch. "Right on the dot."

He offered his arm like the usher at a wedding, and I laughed and took it. "I'm going to be a bridesmaid again," I told him. "And you know what they say about women who are bridesmaids so often." Then I felt furious with myself all over again, for even introducing the subject of weddings.

"They say, 'What a beautiful bridesmaid,'"
Aubrey offered tactfully.

"That's right," I said, relieved. If I couldn't do
better than this, I'd have to keep my mouth shut all
evening.

From my first glimpse of Marcia it was apparent
to me that she lived to entertain. The food even had
little mesh tents over it to keep flies off, a practical
touch in Lawrenceton in the summer. The cloths
covering the tables erected on the sun deck for the
occasion were starched and bright. Marcia was her
usual well-turned-out self, as starched and bright as
the tablecloths in blue cotton shorts and blouse. She
had dangly earrings and painted nails, top and
bottom. She exclaimed over the wine and asked if
we wanted a glass now. We refused politely and she
went in to put it in the refrigerator, while Torrance, looking exceptionally tan in his white shorts
and striped shirt, took our drink orders. We both
took gin and tonics with lots of ice, and went to sit
on the built-in bench that ran all the way around the
huge deck. My feet could barely touch the deck.
Aubrey sat very close when he sat next to me.

Carey and Macon came in right on our heels, and
I introduced them to Aubrey. Macon had met him
before at a ministerial council meeting Macon had
covered for the paper, and they immediately
plunged into an earnest conversation about what
the council hoped to accomplish in the next few

months. Carey eyed my outfit and winked at me, and we talked over the men about how good Marcia and the party food looked. Then the couple who lived in the house across from Carey, the McMans, came up to be introduced, and they assumed that Aubrey and I owned Jane's house together; that we were cohabiting. As we were straightening that out, Lynn and Arthur came in. Lynn was elephantine and obviously very uncomfortable in a maternity shorts outfit. Arthur was looking a little worried and doubtful. When I saw him I felt—nothing.

When Arthur and Lynn worked their way around to us, he seemed to have shaken off whatever had been troubling him. Lynn looked a little more cheerful, too. "I wasn't feeling too well earlier," she confided as Arthur and Aubrey tried to find something to talk about. "But it seems to have stopped for the moment."

"Not good—how?"

"Like gas pains," she said, her mouth a wry twist at this confession. "Honestly, I've never been so miserable in my life. Everything I eat gives me heartburn, and my back is killing me."

"And you're due very soon?"

"Not for a couple more weeks."

"When's your next doctor's appointment?"

"In your last month, you go every week," Lynn said knowledgeably. "I'm due to go back in tomorrow. Maybe he'll tell me something."

I decided I might as well admit wholesale ignorance. Lynn certainly needed something to feel superior about. She had looked sourly on my red and white shorts outfit. "So what could he tell you?" I asked.

"Oh. Well, for example, he could tell me I've started dilating—you know, getting bigger to have the baby. Or he could tell me I'm effacing."

I nodded hastily, so Lynn wouldn't explain what that meant.

"Or how much the baby has dropped, if its head is really far down."

I was sorry I'd asked. But Lynn was looking in better spirits, and she went on to tell Aubrey how they'd decorated the nursery, segueing neatly from that domestic subject to a discussion of the break-ins on the street, which were being generally discussed. The McMans complained about the police inaction on the crimes, unaware that they were about to become very embarrassed.

"You're going to have to understand," Arthur said, his pale blue eyes open wide, which meant he was very irritated, "that if nothing is stolen and no fingerprints are found, and no one sees anything, the burglar is going to be almost impossible to find unless an informant turns in something."

The McMans, small and mousy and shy, turned identical shades of mortification when they realized that the new couple next door were both police detectives. After an embarrassing bumble of apologies and retractions, Carey talked about her break-in—which had occurred when she and her daughter were at Carey's folks' house for Thanksgiving two years ago—and Marcia related her experience, which had "scared her to death."

"I came back from shopping, and of course it was when Torrance was out of town; nothing happens but when Torrance is out of town"—and she gave him a knife of a glance—"and I saw the back window of the kitchen was broken out, oh you should have seen me make tracks over to Jane's house."

"When was that?" I asked. "Around the time Carey's house was broken into?"

"You know, it was. It was maybe a month later. I remember it was cold and we had to get the glass fixed in a hurry."

"When was your house broken into?" I asked Macon, who was holding Carey's hand and enjoying it.

"After the Laverys," he said, after a moment's thought. "They're the people who owned the house you bought," he said to Arthur. "They got transferred five months ago, so I know they're relieved not to have to make two house payments. My break-in, and the Laverys', was like the others...back window, house searched and messed up, but nothing apparently taken."

"When was that?" I persisted. Arthur shot me a sharp look, but Lynn seemed more interested in her stomach, which she was massaging slowly.

"Oh, sometime about a year and a half ago, maybe longer."

"So Jane's house was the only one that hadn't been broken into until very recently?"

Carey, Macon, the McMans, and Marcia and Torrance exchanged glances.

"I think that's right," Macon said. "Come to think of it. And it's been quite awhile since the last one, I know I hadn't thought about it in ages until Carey told me about Jane's house."

"So everyone's been broken into—everyone on the street?" Was that what Jack Burns had told me?

"Well," Marcia said, as she poured dressing on the salad and tossed it, "everyone but the Inces, whose house is on the two lots across from Macon and us. They're very, very old and they never go out anymore. Their daughter-in-law does everything for them, shopping and takes them to doctor appointments and so on. They haven't been bothered, or I'm sure Margie—that's the daughter-in-law— would've come over and told me about it. Every now and then she comes over and has a cup of coffee after she's been to see them."

"I wonder what it means?" I asked no one in particular.

An uncomfortable silence fell.

"Come on, you all, the food's all ready and waiting!" Marcia said cheerfully.

Everyone rose with alacrity except Lynn. I heard Arthur murmur, "You want me to bring you something, hon?"

"Just a little bit," she said wearily. "I'm just not very hungry."

It didn't seem to me that Lynn would have any room left for food, the baby was taking up so much.

Torrance went through the house to answer the front doorbell. The rest of us shuffled through the line, oohing and ahhing appropriately at the gorgeous food. It was presented in a beautiful way, all the dishes decorated and arranged as if far more important people than we were coming to taste it. Unless Marcia had had help, this table represented hours of work. But the food itself was comfortingly homely.

"Barbecued ribs!" exclaimed Aubrey happily. "Oh boy. Roe, you're just going to have to put up with me. I make a mess when I eat them."

"There's not a neat way to eat ribs," I observed. "And Marcia has put out extra large napkins, I see."

"I'd better take two."

Just then I heard a familiar voice rising above the general chatter. I turned to peer around Aubrey, my mouth falling a little open in a foolish way.

"Mother!" I said, in blank surprise.

It was indeed Mother, in elegant cream slacks and midnight blue blouse, impressive but casual gold necklace and earrings, and her new husband in tow.

"I'm so sorry we were late," she was apologizing in her Lauren Bacall gracious woman mode, the one that always made people accept her apology. "John wasn't sure until the last minute whether he felt like coming or not. But I did so want to meet Aurora's new neighbors, and it was so kind of you to invite us..."

The Rideouts gushed back, there was a round of introductions, and suddenly the party seemed livelier and more sophisticated.

Despite his tired eyes, John looked well after their honeymoon, and I told him so. For a few minutes, John seemed a little puzzled as to what exactly Aubrey was doing at the party, but when it sunk in that his minister was my date, John took a deep breath and rose to the occasion, discussing church affairs very briefly with Aubrey, just enough to make them comfortable with each other without boring the non-Episcopalians. Mother and John joined in the food line behind us, Mother sparing a cold glance for Arthur, who was sitting beside his wife and eating while giving her a solicitous look or laying his hand on her shoulder every few seconds.

"She's about to pop. I thought they just got married a few months ago," Mother hissed in my ear.

"Mom, hush," I hissed back.

"I need to talk to you, young lady," Mother responded in a low voice so packed with meaning that I began to wonder what I could have done that she'd heard of. I was almost as nervous as I'd been at six when she used that voice with me.

We sat back down at the picnic tables set with their bright tablecloths and napkins, and Marcia rolled around a cart with drinks and ice on it. She was glowing at all the compliments. Torrance was beaming, too, proud of his wife. I wondered, looking at Lynn and Arthur, why the Rideouts hadn't had children. I wondered if Carey Osland and Macon would try to have another one if they married. Carey was probably forty-two, but women were having them later and later, it seemed. Macon must have been at least six to ten years older than Carey—of course, he had a son who was at least a young adult . . . the missing son.

"While I was in the Bahamas," John said quietly into my ear, "I tried to get a minute to see if the house of Sir Harry Oakes was still standing."

I had to think for a minute. The Oakes case . . . okay, I remembered.

"Alfred de Marigny, acquitted, right?"

"Yes," said John happily. It was always nice to talk to someone who shared your hobby.

"Is this an historical site in the Bahamas?" Aubrey asked from my right.

"Well, in a way," I told him. "The Oakes house was the site of a famous murder." I swung back around to John. "The feathers were the strangest feature of that case, I thought."

"Oh, I think there's an easy explanation," John said dismissively. "I think a fan flew the feathers from a pillow that had been broken open."

"After the fire?"

"Yes, had to have been," John said, wagging his head from side to side. "The feathers looked white in the picture, and otherwise they would've been blackened."

"Feathers?" Aubrey inquired.

"See," I explained patiently, "the body—Sir Harry Oakes—was found partially burned, on a bed, with feathers stuck all over it. The body, I mean, not the bed. Alfred de Marigny, his son-in-law, was charged. But he was acquitted, mostly because of the deplorable investigation by the local police."

Aubrey looked a little—what? I couldn't identify it.

John and I went on happily hashing over the murder of Sir Harry, my mother to John's left carrying on a sporadic conversation with the mousy McMans across from her.

I turned halfway back to Aubrey to make sure he was appreciating a point I was making about the bloody handprint on the screen in the bedroom and noticed he had dropped his ribs on his plate and was looking under the weather.

"What's the matter?" I asked, concerned.

"Would you mind not talking about this particular topic while I eat my ribs, which looked so good until a few minutes ago?" Aubrey was trying to sound jocular, but I could tell he was seriously unhappy with me.

Of course I was at fault. That had the unfortunate result of making me exasperated with Aubrey, as well as myself. I took a few seconds to work myself into a truly penitent frame of mind.

"I'm sorry, Aubrey," I said quietly. I stole a peek at John out of the corner of my eye. He was looking abashed, and my mother had her eyes closed and was silently shaking her head as if her children had tried her beyond her belief, and in public at that. But she quickly rallied and smoothly introduced that neutral and lively subject, the rivalry of the phone companies in the area.

I was so gloomy over my breach of taste that I didn't even chip in my discovery that my phone company could make my phone ring at two houses at the same time. Arthur said he was glad that he had been able to keep his old phone number. I wondered how Lynn felt about giving up her own, but she didn't look as if she gave a damn one way or another. Right after Arthur finished eating and they had thanked Marcia and Torrance in a polite murmur for the party, the good food, and the fellowship, they quietly left to go home.

"That young lady looks uncomfortable," Torrance commented in a lull in the telephone wars. Of course, that led to a discussion of Arthur and Lynn and their police careers, and since I was also a newcomer on the street the discussion moved logically to my career, which I was obliged to tell them—including my mother—had come to an end.

I thought if my mother's face held its mildly interested smile any longer, it would crack.

Aubrey had finished his supper finally and joined in the conversation, but in a subdued way. I thought we were going to have to talk sometime soon about my interest in murder cases and the fact that he found them nauseating. I was trying not to think about how much fun it had been to talk to John about the fascinating Oakes case...and it had occurred while the duke and duchess of Windsor were governing the islands! I'd have to catch my new stepfather alone sometime and we could really hash it over.

I was recalled to the here and now by my mother's voice in my ear. "Come to the bathroom for a moment!"

I excused myself and went in the house with her. I'd never been in the Rideouts' before, and I could only gather an impression of spotless maintenance and bright colors before I was whisked into the hall bathroom. It seemed like a teenager sort of thing to do, going into the bathroom together, and just as I opened my mouth to ask my mother if she had a date to the prom, she turned to me after locking the door and said—

"What, young woman, is a skull doing in my blanket bag?"

FOR WHAT FELT LIKE the tenth time in one day I was left with my mouth hanging open. Then I rallied.

"What on earth were you doing getting a blanket out in this weather?"

"Getting a blanket for my husband while he was having chills with the flu," she told me through clenched teeth. "Don't you dare try to sidetrack me!"

"I found it," I said.

"Great. So you found a human skull, and you decided to put it in a blanket bag in your mother's house while she was out of town. That makes perfect sense. A very rational procedure."

I was going to have to level with her. But locked in Marcia Rideout's bathroom was not the situation.

"Mom, I swear that tomorrow I'll come to your house and tell you all about it."

"I'm sure any time would be okay with you because you have no job to go to," my mother said very politely. "However, I have to earn my living, and I am going to work. I will expect you to be at my house tomorrow night at seven o'clock, when I had better hear a good explanation for what you have done. And while I'm saying drastic things, I might as well tell you something else, though since you have been an adult I have tried not to give you any advice on your affairs of the heart—or whatever. Do *not* sleep with my husband's minister. It would be very embarrassing for John."

"For John? It would be embarrassing for *John*?" Get a hold, I told myself. I took a deep breath, looked in the gleaming mirror, and pushed my glasses up on my nose. "Mother, I can't tell you how glad I am that you have restrained yourself, all these years, from commenting on my social life, other than telling me you wished I had more of one."

We looked at each other in the mirror with stormy eyes. Then I tried smiling at her. She tried smiling at me. The smiles were tiny, but they held.

"All right," she said finally, in a more moderate voice. "We'll see you tomorrow night."

"It's a date," I agreed.

When we came back to the sun deck, the party had swung around to the bones found at the end of the street. Carey was saying the police had been to ask her if there was anything she remembered that might help to identify the bones as her husband's. "I told them," she was saying, "that that rascal had run off and left me, not been killed. For weeks after he didn't come back, I thought he might walk back through that door with those diapers. You know," she told Aubrey parenthetically, "he left to get diapers for the baby and never came back." Aubrey nodded, perhaps to indicate understanding or perhaps because he'd already heard this bit of Lawrenceton folklore. "When the police found the car at the Amtrak station," Carey continued, "I knew he'd just run off. He's been dead to me ever since, but I definitely don't believe those bones are his." Macon put his arm around her. The mousy McMans were enthralled at this real-life drama. My mother stared at me in sudden consternation. I pretended I didn't see it.

"So I told them he'd broken his leg once, the year before we got married, if that would tell them anything, and they thanked me and said they'd let me know. But after the first day he was gone, when I was so distraught; well, after the police told me they'd found his car, I didn't worry about him anymore. I just felt mad."

Carey had gotten upset, and was trying very hard not to let a tear roll down her cheeks. Marcia Rideout was staring at her, hoping her party was not going to be ruined by a guest weeping openly.

Torrance said soothingly, "Now, Carey, it's not Mike, it's some old tramp. That's sad, but it's nothing for us to worry about." He stood, holding his drink, his sturdy body and calm voice somehow immensely reassuring.

Everyone seemed to relax a little. But then Marcia said, "But where's the skull? On this evening's television news they said there wasn't a skull." Her hand was shaking as she put the lid on a casserole. "Why wasn't the head there?"

It was a tense moment. I couldn't help clenching my drink tighter and looking down at the deck. My mother's eyes were on me; I could feel her glare.

"It sounds macabre," Aubrey said gently, "but perhaps a dog or some other animal carried off the skull. There's no reason it couldn't have been with the rest of the body for some time."

"That's true," Macon said after a moment's consideration.

The tension eased again. After a little more talk, my mother and John rose to leave. No one is immune to my mother's graciousness; Marcia and Torrance were beaming by the time she made her progress out the front door, John right behind her basking in the glow. The McMans soon said they had to pay off their baby-sitter and take her home, since it was a school night. Carey Osland, too, said she had to relieve her sitter. "Though my daughter is beginning to think she can stay by herself," she told us proudly. "But for now she definitely needs someone there, even when I'm just two houses away."

"She's an independent girl," Macon said with a smile. He seemed quite taken with Carey's daughter. "I'd only been around boys before, and girls are so different to raise. I hope I can do a better job helping Carey than I did raising my son."

Since the Rideouts were childless, and so was I, and so was Aubrey, we had no response that would have made sense.

I thanked Marcia for the party, and complimented her and Torrance on the decorations and food.

"Well, I did barbecue the ribs," Torrance admitted, running his hand over his already bristly chin, "but all the rest of the fixing is Marcia's work."

I told Marcia she should be a caterer, and she flushed with pleasure. She looked just like a department store mannequin with a little pink painted on the cheeks for realism, so pretty and so perfect.

"Every hair is in place," I told Aubrey wonderingly as we walked over to his car parked in my driveway. "She wouldn't ever let her hair do this," and I sunk my hands into my own flyaway mop.

"That's what I want to do," Aubrey said promptly, and, stopping and facing me, he ran his hands through my hair. "It's beautiful," he said in an unministerly voice.

Woo-woo. The kiss that followed was long and thorough enough to remind me of exactly how long it had been since I had biblically known anyone. I could tell Aubrey felt the same.

We mutually disengaged. "I shouldn't have done that," Aubrey said. "It makes me..."

"Me, too," I agreed, and he laughed, and the mood was broken. I was very glad I hadn't worn the orange-and-white dress. Then his hands would have been on my bare back.... I started to chatter to distract myself. We leaned against his car, talking about the party, my new stepfather's flu, my quitting my job, his retreat for priests he'd be attending that Friday and Saturday at a nearby state park.

"Shall I follow you home?" he asked, as he slid into his car.

"I might spend the night here," I said. I bent in and gave him a light kiss on the lips and a smile, and then he left.

I walked to the kitchen door and went in. The moon through the open kitchen curtains gave me plenty of light, so I went to the bedroom in darkness. The contrast of quiet and dark with the talk, talk, talk I'd done that day made me sleepier than a pill would have. I switched on the bathroom light briefly to brush my teeth and shuck my clothes. Then I pulled the rose pink nightgown over my head, switched off the bathroom light, and made my way to the bed in darkness. To the quiet hum of the air-conditioning and the occasional tiny mew from the kittens in the closet, I fell fast asleep.

TWELVE

I WOKE UP. I knew where I was instantly—in Jane's house. I swung my legs over the side of the bed automatically, preparing to trek to the bathroom. But I realized in a slow, middle-of-the-night way that I didn't need to go.

The cats were quiet.

So why was I awake?

Then I heard movement somewhere else in the house, and saw a beam of light flash through the hall. Someone was in the house with me. I bit the insides of my mouth together to keep from screaming.

Jane's clock-radio on the bedside table had a glowing face that illuminated the outline of the bedside phone. With fingers that were almost useless, I lifted the receiver, taking such care, such care... no noise. Thank God it was a push-button. From instinct I dialed the number I knew so well, the number that would bring help even faster than 911.

"Hello?" said a voice in my ear, groggy with sleep.

"Arthur," I breathed. "Wake up."

"Who is this?"

"It's Roe. I'm across the street in Jane's house. There is someone in the house."

"I'll be there in a minute. Stay quiet. Hide."

I hung up the phone so gently, so delicately, trying to control my hands, oh Lord, let me not make a sound.

I knew what had given me away, it was my downward glance when the skull was mentioned, at the party. Someone had been watching for just such a reaction.

I slid my glasses on while I was thinking. I had two options on hiding: under the bed or in the closet with the cats. The intruder was in the guest bedroom, just a short hall length away. I could see the flashlight beam bobbing here and there; searching, searching again, for the damn *skull*! The best place to hide would be the big dirty-clothes closet in the bathroom; I was small enough to double up in there, since it was almost square to match the linen closet on top of it. If I hid in the bedroom closet, the intruder might hear the cat noises and investigate. But I couldn't risk slipping into the bathroom now, with the light flashing in the hallway unpredictably.

In response to my thoughts, it seemed, the light bobbed out of the guest bedroom, into the little hall, through the big archway into the living room.

When it was well within the living room, I slid off the bed onto my feet with the tiniest of thumps...

...and landed right on Madeleine's tail. The cat yowled, I screamed, a startled exclamation came from the living room. I heard thumping footsteps and, when a blob was in the doorway, pausing, maybe fumbling for a light switch, I leaped. I hit someone right in the chest, wrapped my right arm around a beefy neck, and with my left hand grabbed a handful of short hair and pulled as hard as I could. Something from a self-defense course I'd taken popped into my mind and I began shrieking at the top of my lungs.

Something hit me a terrible blow on the back, but I tightened my grip on the short hair and my stranglehold on the neck. "Stop," wheezed a heavy voice, "stop, stop!" And blows began raining on my back and legs. I was being shaken loose by all the staggering and my own weight, and I had to stop screaming to catch my breath. But I sucked it in and had opened my mouth to shriek again when the lights came on.

My attacker whirled to face the person who'd turned on the light, and in that whirl I was slung off onto the floor, landing not quite on my feet and staggering into the bedpost to collect a few more bruises.

Lynn Liggett Smith stood leaning against the wall in the hall, breathing heavily, the gun in her hand pointing at Torrance Rideout, who had only a flashlight dangling from his hand. If the flashlight had been a knife, I'd have been bleeding from a dozen wounds; as it was, I felt like Lee's Army had marched over me. I held on to the bedpost and panted. Where was Arthur?

Torrance took in Lynn's weak stance and huge belly and turned back to me.

"You have to tell me," he said desperately, as if she wasn't even there, "you have to tell me where the skull is."

"Put your hands against the wall," Lynn said steadily but weakly. "I'm a police officer and I will shoot."

"You're nine months pregnant and about to fall down," Torrance said over his shoulder. He turned to me again. *"Where is the skull?"* His broad, open face was crossed with seams I'd never noticed before, and there was blood trickling down from his scalp onto his white shirt. I seemed to have removed a square inch of hair.

Lynn fired into the ceiling.

"Put your hands against the wall, you bastard," she said coldly.

And he did.

He hadn't realized that if Lynn really shot at him she stood an excellent chance of hitting me. Before he got the idea, I moved to the other side of the bed. But then I couldn't see Lynn. This bedroom was too tight. I didn't like Torrance being between me and the door.

"Roe," Lynn said from the hall, slowly. "Pat him down and see if he's got a gun. Or a knife." She sounded like she was in pain.

I hated getting so close to Torrance. Did he respect the gun enough? Had he picked up on the strain in Lynn's voice? I wished, for a moment, that she had gone on and shot him.

My only ideas about patting a suspect down came from television. I had a shrinking distaste for touching Torrance's body, but I pursed my lips and ran my hands over him.

"Just change in his pocket," I said hoarsely. My screaming had hurt more than Torrance's ears.

"Okay," said Lynn slowly. "Here are the cuffs."

When I looked right in her face, I was shocked. Her eyes were wide and frightened, she was biting her lower lip. The gun was steady in her hand, but it was taking all her will to keep it so. The carpet looked dark around her feet, which were wearing slippers that were dark and light pink. I looked more closely. The darkness on her slippers was wetness. She had fluid trickling down her legs. There was a funny smell in the air. Lynn's water had broken.

Where was Arthur?

I closed my eyes for a second in sheer consternation. When I opened them, Lynn and I were staring at each other in panic. Then Lynn hardened her glare and said, "Take the cuffs, Roe."

I reached through the narrow doorway and took them. Arthur had shown me how to use his one day, so I did know how to close them on Torrance's wrists.

"Hold out your hands behind you," I said as viciously as I could. Lynn and I were going to lose control any minute. I'd gotten one cuff on when Torrance erupted. He swung the arm with the cuff on it around, and the flying loose cuff caught me on the side of the head. But he mustn't get the gun! I gripped whatever of him I could grab, blinded by pain, and hobbled him enough to land us both on the floor, rolling around in the limited space, me hanging on for my own dear life, him desperately trying to be rid of me.

"Torrance, stop!" shrieked yet another voice, and we were still, him on top of me panting and me underneath barely breathing at all. Past his shoulder I could see Marcia, her hair still smooth, her blue shorts and shirt obviously hastily pulled on.

"Honey, it doesn't make any difference anymore, we have to stop," she said gently. He got off me to swing around and look at her heavily. Then Lynn moaned, a terrible sound.

Torrance seemed mesmerized by his wife. I crawled past him and past her, actually brushing her leg as I went by. They both ignored me in the eeriest way.

Lynn had slid down the wall. She was making a valiant attempt to hold the gun up but couldn't manage anymore. When she saw me, her eyes made an appeal and her hand fell to the floor and released the gun. I took it and swung around, fully intending to somehow shoot both the Rideouts, our recent hosts. But they were still wrapped up in each other, and I could have riddled them both for all they paid attention to me. With the affronted feeling of being a child whose anger adults won't take seriously, I turned back to Lynn.

Her eyes were closed, and her breathing was funny. Then I realized she was breathing in a pattern.

"You're having the baby," I said sadly.

She nodded, still with her eyes closed, and kept her breathing going.

"You called some backup, right?"

She nodded again.

"Arthur must have been out on a call; that was you on the phone," I observed, and I went into the bathroom right at my back to wash my hands and get some towels.

"I don't know nothin' 'bout birthin' no babies," I told my reflection, pushed my glasses up on my nose, had the fleeting thought that it was nothing short of amazing they hadn't been cracked, and went to squat by Lynn's side. I gingerly pulled up her nightgown and lay towels on the floor beneath her drawn-up knees.

"Where is the skull?" Torrance asked me. His voice sounded defeated.

"At my mom's house in a closet," I said briefly, my attention absorbed by Lynn.

"So Jane had it all the time," he said, in a wooden voice from which all the wonder was leached. "That old woman had it all the time. She was furious after the tree thing, you know. I couldn't believe it, all those years we were good neighbors, then there was this trouble about the damn tree. Next thing I know, there was a hole in the yard and the head was gone. But I never connected the two things. I even left Jane's house for last because I thought she was least likely to have it."

"Oh, Torrance," Marcia said pitifully. "I wish you had told me. Was it you who broke into all the houses?"

"Looking for the head," he said. "I knew someone around here had to have it, but it never occurred to me it could be Jane. It had to be someone who could have seen me burying him, but not Jane, not that sweet little old lady. I just knew that if she'd seen me burying him, she'd have called the police. And I had to wait," Torrance meandered on, "so long between each house, because after each break-in, people would be so cautious for a long time..."

"You even pretended to break into our house," marveled his wife.

Gingerly I stole a peek under the nightgown. I was instantly sorry.

"Lynn," I told her hesitantly, "I see what I think is the baby's head, I guess."

Lynn nodded emphatically. Her eyes flew open, and she focused on a point on the wall opposite. Her breathing became ragged for a few moments. "Get yourself together!" I said earnestly. Lynn was the only person who knew what was happening. Lynn seemed to take that as advice offered from compassion, and squeezed my hand till I thought of screaming again.

Suddenly she caught her breath, and her whole body tensed.

I peeked again.

"Oh dear," I breathed. This was really quite a lot worse than watching Madeleine the cat. I followed my own advice and pulled myself together, despite my desire to run screaming out of this house and never come back. I let go of Lynn's hand and moved between her legs. There was barely room. It was lucky I was a small person.

Lynn strained again.

"Okay, Lynn," I said bracingly. "It's coming. I'll catch it."

Lynn seemed to rest for a moment.

"Whose skull?" I asked Torrance. Marcia had sunk to the floor, and they were sitting knee to knee holding hands.

"Oh," he said as if he'd lost interest. "The skull is Mark. Mark Kaplan. The boy who rented our apartment."

Lynn gathered herself and pushed again. Her eyes were glazed, and I was scared to death. I hesitantly put my hands where they might do some good.

"Lynn, I see more of the head," I told her.

Amazingly, Lynn smiled. And she gathered herself. And pushed.

"I've got the head, Lynn," I told her in a shaky voice. I was trying to sound confident, but I failed. Would the baby's neck break if I let its head flop? Oh dear Jesus, I needed help, I was so inadequate.

Lynn did it again.

"That's the shoulders," I whispered, holding this tiny, bloody, vulnerable thing. "One more push should do it," I said bracingly, having no idea at all what I was talking about. But it seemed to hearten Lynn, and she started pulling herself together again. I wished that she could take a break, so I could, but I had told her the truth out of sheer ignorance. Lynn pushed like she was in the Olympics of baby extrusion, and the slippery thing shot out of her like a hurtling football, or so it seemed to me. And I caught it.

"What?" asked Lynn weakly.

It took me a second of sheer stupidity to understand her. I should be doing something! I should make it cry! Wasn't that important?

"Hold it upside down and whack it on its back," Marcia said. "That's what they do on TV."

Full of terror, I did so. The baby let out a wail. So it was breathing, it was alive! So far so good. Though still hooked up to Lynn, this child was okay for now. Should I do something to the umbilical cord? What? And I heard sirens coming, thank the Lord.

"What?" Lynn asked more urgently.

"Girl!" I said jerkily. "A girl!" I held the little thing as I had seen babies held in pictures and made plans to burn the rose pink nightgown.

"Well," said Lynn with a tiny smile, as pounding began on the front door, "damn if I'm going to name it after you."

IT TOOK SOME TIME to sort out the situation in Jane's little house, which seemed more crowded than ever with all the policemen in Lawrenceton.

Some of the policemen, seeing Arthur's former flame kneeling before his new wife, both bloody, assumed I was the person to arrest. They could hardly put cuffs on me or search me, though, since

I was holding the baby, who was still attached to Lynn. And when they all realized I was holding a newborn baby and not some piece I'd ripped from Lynn's insides, they went nuts. No one seemed to remember that there'd been a break-in, that consequently the burglar might be on the scene.

Arthur had been out on a robbery call, but when he arrived he was so scared he was ready to kill someone. He waved his gun around vaguely, and when he spotted Lynn and the blood he began bellowing "Ambulance! Ambulance!" Jack Burns himself pushed right by the Rideouts to use the phone in the bedroom.

Arthur was by me in a flash, babbling. "The baby!" he said. He didn't know what to do with his gun.

"Put the gun away and take this baby," I said rather sharply. "It's still attached to Lynn, and I don't know what to do about that."

"Lynn, how are you?" Arthur said in a daze.

"Honey, put a towel over your suit and take your daughter," Lynn said weakly.

"My—oh." He holstered his gun and reached down and took a towel off the stack I'd brought out. I wondered if Jane could ever have imagined her monogrammed white cotton towels being used for such a purpose. I handed the baby over with alacrity, and stood up, trembling from a cocktail of fear, pain, and shock. I was more than glad to vacate my position between Lynn's legs.

One of the ambulance attendants ran up to me then and said, "You the maternity? Or have you been injured?"

I pointed a shaky finger at Lynn. I didn't blame him for thinking I'd been seriously hurt; I was covered with smears of blood, some of it Lynn's, some of it Torrance's, a little of it mine.

"Are you all right?"

I looked to the source of the voice and found I was standing next to Torrance. This was so strange.

"I'll be okay," I said wearily.

"I'm sorry. I was never cut out to be a criminal."

I thought of the inept break-ins, Torrance not even taking anything to make them look like legitimate burglaries. I nodded.

"Why did you do it?" I asked him.

Suddenly his face hardened and tightened all over. "I just did," he said.

"So when Jane dug up the skull, you dug up the rest of the body and put the bones by the dead end sign?"

"I knew no one would clean up that brush for years," he said. "And I was right. I was too scared to carry the bones in my trunk, even for a little while. I waited till the next night when Macon went over to Carey's, and I carried the bones in a plastic bag through his backyard and up the far side of his house; then it was just a few feet to the brush...no one saw me *that* time. I was so sure whoever had taken the skull would call the police. I waited. Then I realized whoever had the skull just wanted...to have it. For me to squirm. I had almost forgotten that trouble about the tree. Jane was so ladylike. I never believed ..."

"And he never told me about it," said Marcia, to his left. "He never let me worry, too." She looked at him fondly.

"So, what did you do it for?" I asked Torrance. "Did he make a pass at Marcia?"

"Well...," said Torrance hesitantly.

"Oh, honey," Marcia said reproving. She leaned over to me, smiling a little at a man's silly gesture. "He didn't do it," she told me. "I did it."

"You killed Mark Kaplan and buried him out in the yard?"

"Oh, Torrance buried him when I told him what I'd done."

"Oh," I said inadequately, swallowed by her wide blue eyes. "You killed him because—?"

"He came over while Torrance was gone." She shook her head sadly as she told me. "And I had thought he was such a nice person. But he *wasn't*. He was very dirty."

I nodded, just to be responding somehow.

"Mike Osland, too," Marcia ran on, still shaking her head at the perfidy of men.

I felt suddenly very, very cold. Torrance closed his eyes in profound weariness.

"Mike," I murmured interrogatively.

"He's under the sun deck, that's why Torrance built it, I think," Marcia said earnestly. "Jane didn't know about him."

"She's confessing," said an incredulous hoarse voice.

I turned from Marcia's mesmerizing eyes to see that Jack Burns was sitting on his haunches in front of me.

"Did she just confess to a murder?" he asked me.

"Two," I said.

"Two murders," he repeated. He took his turn at head shaking. I would have to find someone at whom I could shake *my* head incredulously. "She just confessed two murders to you. How do *you do it*?"

Faced by his round, hot eyes, I became aware that I was in a torn and disheveled and rather skimpy-at-the-top nightgown that had become quite soiled in the course of the night. I was definitely reminded that I was not Jack Burns's favorite person. I wondered how much Lynn would remember of what she'd overheard while she was having the baby—was it possible she would remember my telling Torrance that I knew the whereabouts of the skull?

Lynn was being carried out on a stretcher now. I presumed that the afterbirth had been delivered and disposed of. I hoped I wouldn't find it on the bathroom floor or something.

"This man," I told Jack Burns, as I pointed to Torrance, "broke into my house tonight."

"Are you hurt?" asked Sergeant Burns, with reluctant professional solicitude.

I turned to look in Torrance Rideout's eyes. "No," I said clearly. "Not at all. And I have no idea why he broke in here or what he was looking for."

Torrance's eyes showed a slow recognition. And, to my amazement, he winked at me when Jack Burns turned away to call his cohorts over.

After an eternity, every single person was gone from Jane's house but me, its owner. What do you do after a night you've had a burglary, been battered, delivered a baby, and nearly been mown down by the entire detective force of Lawrenceton, Georgia? Also, I continued enumerating as I hauled the remains of the nightgown over my head, heard a confession of double murder and had your scarcely covered bosom ogled by the same detectives who had been about to mow you down minutes earlier?

Well. I was going to take a hot, hot bath to soak my bruises and strains. I was going to calm a nearly berserk Madeleine, who was crouching in a corner of the bedroom closet hoping she was concealed underneath a blanket I'd thrown in there. Madeleine, as it happened, did not react well to home invasion. Then, possibly, I could put my tired carcass back between the cool sheets and sleep a little.

There'd be hell to pay in the morning.

My mother would call.

BUT I ONLY SLEPT four hours. When I woke it was eight o'clock, and I lay in bed and thought for a moment.

Then I was up and brushing my teeth, pulling back on my shorts set from the night before. I managed to get a brush through my hair, which had been damp from the tub when I'd fallen asleep the night before. I let Madeleine out and back in—she seemed calm again—and then it was time to get to Wal-Mart.

I walked in as the doors were unlocked and found what I was looking for after a talk with a salesperson.

I stopped in at the town house and got out my box of gift wrap.

At Mother's house both cars were gone. I'd finally gotten a break. I used my key one last time; I never would again now that John lived here, too. I sped up the stairs and got the old blanket bag out of the closet and left the gift-wrapped blanket bag on the kitchen table on my way out. I left my key by it.

Quickly out to my car then, and speeding back to the house on Honor.

Another stroke of luck; no police cars at the Rideouts' yet.

I went out the back kitchen door and looked around as carefully as Torrance Rideout must have the night he buried Mark Kaplan, the night he buried Mike Osland. But this was daylight, far more dangerous. I'd counted cars as I pulled into my own driveway: Lynn's car was at the house across the street, Arthur's was gone. That figured; he was at the hospital with his wife and his baby.

I did falter then. But I reached up and slapped myself on the cheek. This was no time to get weepy.

The elderly Inces were not a consideration. I peered over to Carey Osland's house. Her car was home. She must have been told of the confession by Marcia Rideout that Mike Osland was in the Rideouts' backyard. I could only hope that Carey didn't decide to come look personally.

As I started across my backyard, I had to smother an impulse to crouch and run, or slither on my belly. The pink blanket bag seemed so conspicuous. But I just couldn't bring myself to open it and carry the bare skull in my hands. Besides, I'd already rubbed my prints off. I got to the sun deck with no one shouting, "Hey! What are you doing?" and took a few deep breaths. Now hurry, I told myself, and unzipped the bag, grabbed the thing inside by hooking a finger through the jaw, and, trying not to look at it, I rolled it as far as I could under the deck. I was tempted to climb the steps to the deck, look between the boards, and see if the skull showed from on top. But instead I turned and walked quickly back to my own yard, praying that no one had noticed my strange behavior. I was still clutching the zip bag. Once inside, I glanced in the bag to check that no traces were left of the skull's presence, and folded one of Jane's blankets, zipped it inside, and shoved the bag to the back of the shelf in one of the guest bedroom closets. Then I sat at the little table in the kitchen, and out the window toward the Rideouts' I saw men starting to take apart the sun deck.

I had just made it.

I shook all over. I put my head in my hands and cried.

After a while, that seemed to dry up, and I felt limp and tired. I made a pot of coffee and sat at the table and drank it while I watched the men demolish the deck and find the skull. After the hubbub that caused was over and after the skull had been placed carefully in a special bag of some kind (which actually made me smile a little), the men began digging. It was hot, and they all sweated, and I saw Sergeant Burns glance over to my house as though he'd like to come ask me a few questions, but I'd answered them all the night before. All I was ever going to answer.

Then one of the men gave a shout, and the others gathered round, and I decided maybe I wouldn't watch anymore. At noon the phone rang, and it was my mother, thanking me crisply for the lovely new blanket storage bag and reminding me that we were going to eat dinner together and have a long talk.

"Sure, Mom," I said, and sighed. I was sore and stiff; maybe she would cut it short. "Mom, tomorrow I'm going to come in and list this house."

Well, that was business. That was different. Or maybe not. "I'll list it myself," she promised meaningfully, and hung up.

The phone was on the wall by the letter rack and the calendar, a sensible and convenient arrangement. I stood staring blankly at the letter rack for a few seconds, finally taking down a charity appeal, pulling out the begging letter, looking it over, throwing it away. I took out another letter, which should have been a bill from the bug-spray people by the envelope...why didn't Bubba Sewell have it? He should have all the bills. But the stamp had been canceled months before.

Suddenly I knew what this was, knew even as I shook the paper out of the slit that it was not going to be a bill from Orkin.

Of course: "The Purloined Letter." Jane liked *classics*.

"On a Wednesday night in the summer, four years ago," the letter began abruptly,

I, Jane Engle, was sitting in my backyard. It was very late because I had insomnia, and I often sit in the garden in the dark when I have insomnia. It was about midnight, when I saw Mark Kaplan, the Rideouts' boarder, go to Marcia's back door and knock. I could see him clearly in the floodlight the Rideouts have at their back door. Marcia always leaves it on all night when Torrance is out of town. Marcia came to the door, and Mark Kaplan, right away, attacked her. I believe he had been drinking, that he had a bottle in his hand, but I am not sure. Before I could go to her help, she somehow knocked him down, and I saw her grab something from her kitchen counter and hit Mark Kaplan on the back of the head with it. I am not sure what she picked up, but I think it was a hammer. Then I became aware another car had pulled up into the Rideouts' carport, and realized that Torrance had come home.

I went inside, thinking that soon I would hear police cars and I would have to talk to the police about what I'd seen. So I changed into my regular clothes—I'd had my nightgown on—and sat in the kitchen and waited in the dark for something to happen.

Instead of police cars, sirens, and whatnot, I saw Torrance come out in a few minutes with a tablecloth. Clearly something body size was wrapped in it, and I was sure it was Mark Kaplan. Torrance proceeded over to their old garden plot, and began to dig. I stayed awake the rest of the night, watching him. I didn't call the police, though I gave it some thought. I knew what testifying in court could do to Marcia Rideout, who has never been any too stable. Also, Mark Kaplan did attack her, and I knew it.

So I said nothing.

But a little over a year and a half later, I got into a dispute with Torrance over my tree, from which he arrogantly trimmed some branches. Every time I looked out my kitchen window, the tree looked worse. So I did something I'm not proud of. I waited till the Rideouts were both out of town, and I went over in the night and dug where I'd seen Torrance dig many months before. It took me three nights, since I am an old woman, but I reached the skull. I removed it and brought it home with me. And I left the hole open, to be sure Torrance knew someone had the head, someone knew.

I am truly not proud of this. Now I am too sick to put the skull back, and I am too afraid of Torrance to just give it to him. And I have been thinking of Mike Osland; he disappeared before Mark Kaplan was killed, and I remember seeing him look at Marcia at parties. I think now that Marcia, just a little eccentric on the surface, is actually quite disturbed, and I think Torrance knows this; and yet he goes on with his life as though by denying she needs special care, she will get better.

I am too close to my own death to worry about this anymore. If my lawyer finds this, he must do as he thinks best: I don't care what people say about me when I am gone. If Roe finds this, she must do as pleases her. The skull is in the window seat.

                                        Jane Engle

I looked down at the paper in my hands, then refolded it. Without really considering it, I began shredding the letter, first in halves, then quarters, then thirds, until finally I had a little pile of confetti on the counter. I gathered it all up and dropped it down the sink, running the water and starting the disposal. After it had rumbled for a moment, I turned off the water and carefully checked all the other letters in the rack. They were exactly what they seemed.

I looked at Jane's calendar, still turned to two months before. I took it down and flipped it to the right page and hung it back up. It was perfectly blank. The strangest thing about not having a job was that it made the whole week so shapeless. I wasn't even taking a day off from anything. Suddenly emptiness spread out in front of me like a slippery ramp. Surely there was something I had to do?

Sure there was. I shook my head in horror. I'd almost forgotten that today was the day I was supposed to pick up my altered bridesmaid's dress.

Miss Joe Nell would have had a fit if I'd forgotten.

And then I knew what I'd do tomorrow.

I'd start looking for my own house.

I detoured by the cemetery on my way to Great Day. I walked up the little hill to Jane's headstone, already in place. If Bubba Sewell could get things done that fast, perhaps he was worth voting for. Feeling stupid and sentimental, I stared at the headstone for a few seconds. This had been a dumb idea. Finally, I said, "Okay, I'm going to enjoy it."

I hadn't come out to the cemetery to do this. I could've talked to Jane from anywhere. A trickle of sweat tickled my spine. "Thanks a lot," I said, hoping I didn't sound sarcastic. "But don't do me any more favors," I told the stone, and began laughing.

I got back in my car and went to pick up the bridesmaid's dress.

A DEB RALSTON MYSTERY

HACKER

First Time in Paperback

 LEE MARTIN

OVERKILL

Hovering perilously near burnout with the demands of police duty and family life—specifically toddler, husband, teenager and a friend comatose from a hit-and-run—Fort Worth detective Deb Ralston now adds a grisly ax murder to her twenty-five-hour days.

A man and his computer are hacked to pieces. Eric Huffman had no enemies, no reason to be so violently murdered. The evidence is thin, but disturbing...since the pattern seems poised to repeat itself in Deb's own household.

"Martin continues the fine work begun in the earlier *Deficit Ending* and *The Mensa Murders*..." —*Booklist*

Available in January at your favorite retail stores.

 WØRLDWIDE LIBRARY®

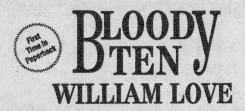
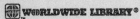

Caught in the Shadows

C. A. Haddad

First Time in Paperback

STRANGER THAN FICTION

Hacking may be borderline legal, but the profit is there, big-time, especially in a high-profile divorce case such as the one Chicago computer "researcher" Becky Belski has just been handed.

Arrest record? Bank statement? Charges? If it's in a computer network, Becky can find it. What she didn't expect to find was a link to her own murky half-forgotten past...and the murder of her stepfather.

An open-and-shut case convicted Becky's mother more than twenty years ago. Now Becky is certain that the wrong person went to jail. Between hacking away at the past and juggling two men, she finally discovers the shocking truth.

"The hallmark of the C. A. Haddad mysteries...is that they're sassy, sexy and very funny."—*Publishers Weekly*

Available in February at your favorite retail stores.

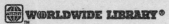
WORLDWIDE LIBRARY ®

CAUGHT

First Time in Paperback

THE *Devil* DOWN HOME

A SAM AND NICKY TITUS MYSTERY

EVE K. SANDSTROM

ALL HALLOW'S EVIL

Spotting Dracula hitchhiking at the side of the road, Sheriff Sam Titus and his wife, Nicky, do the neighborly thing—give him a lift. Black cloak and deathly pallor aside, the stranger's name is Damon Revels, and his business in Holton goes back fifteen years.

But trick or treat turns deadly when Damon's body is found in a coffin at the local Haunted House fund-raiser. Surrounding the knife protruding from his chest is a pentagram—the mark of devil worshipers. A human sacrifice?

Then another murder with satanic trimmings occurs, and terror is mounting. Whether it actually is a cult or the work of a clever killer, Sam and Nicky are now hunting the devil down home.

"I'm looking forward to more from Nicky and Sam...a fun, quick read."
—*Mystery News*

Available in March at your favorite retail stores.